HARRY

Glen R Stansfield

All the best
Glen R Stansfield

The Man in a Hat
7 St John Street, Creetown, Newton Stewart DG8 7JA
Copyright © 2016 Glen R Stansfield
Glen R Stansfield has asserted his right to be identified as the author of this work.
British spelling is used throughout.
This book is a work of fiction and, except in the case of historical fact, any resemblance to actual persons, living or dead, is purely coincidental.
All rights reserved. No part of this publication may be reproduced, stored in a retrieval system, or transmitted, in any form or by any means, without the prior permission in writing of the Publisher, or as expressly permitted by law, by licence or under terms agreed with the appropriate reprographics rights organisation. Enquiries concerning reproduction outside the scope of the above should be sent to the Publisher, at the address above.
This book is sold subject to the condition that it shall not, by way of trade or otherwise, be lent, resold, hired out, or otherwise circulated without the publisher's prior consent in any form of binding or cover other than that with which it is published and without similar condition, including this condition being imposed on the subsequent purchaser.

ISBN: 978-0-9933118-3-3

Printed by Lightning Source,
Great Britain, United States and Australia,
Business International, Bahrain
CreateSpace, Charleston, SC

HARRY

To my loving wife, Jess

John Harrison was dead. His body and mind were not aware of it yet, but the moment he broke into the church his death became inevitable. Some would say it was the hand of God, many would say it was deserved, few would mourn his passing.

Had he chosen a different path he may have lived, but fate brought him to this place at this precise moment, and John Harrison ceased to be.

Acknowledgements

These are the people that in one way or another made this book possible. My thanks go to the following, and I hope I have not forgotten anyone;

Rob Jeffries, (Hon. Curator, Thames Police Museum, Wapping.)
Vikkie Mulford, (Collections Assistant, Chatham Historic Dockyard Trust.)
Charles Henty, Esq. (Secondary of London and Under Sheriff High Bailiff of Southwark Central Criminal Court, Old Bailey.)
Sue Noyes for her unceasing proofreading and editing.
Seumas Gallacher, for his continuing encouragement and invaluable advice.

And not least my wife Jess, who still has to listen to my prattlings.

HARRY

2016

CHAPTER ONE

The sight of a white tarpaulin spanning the width of the railway arch greeted the early morning joggers and walkers on the towpath opposite. A crime scene tent connected with it on one side of the bridge. Above, the trains on the Dockland's Light Railway continued their daily shuttle of commuters. Tomorrow, the murder would be front page news, but for today the passengers remain oblivious to the scene beneath them, safely cocooned in their own little world, reading yesterday's news.

A constable, armed with a clipboard and pen, stood in front of the 'Police' tape stretched across the adjacent street and kept the non-existent onlookers at bay. On the far side of the canal, along the increasingly busy towpath, a brightly coloured line of narrow boats lay moored, and a small crowd of residents and passers-by gathered to watch the grim proceedings, but the majority of people passing along the canal remained engrossed in their daily routines, paying no heed to the activity on the far bank; none of this mattered to them.

Two figures emerged from a recently parked car, donned white, disposable crime-scene suits then stepped

ONE

briskly towards the tape. The constable noted their details on his clipboard before allowing them through; every person entering logged in and out. Trace evidence at the scene that couldn't be attributed to the investigators may belong to a perpetrator. The crime-scene suits reduced the possibility of contamination. Everyone entering had to wear one, properly fastened; unlike the TV where detectives wandered willy-nilly, trampling on the evidence, prodding this and poking that, finally unearthing the vital clue that cracked the case; a clue the SOCO team had so conveniently overlooked, despite their many hours of hard work. In the real world, the scene would be managed from start to finish, methodically, cataloguing and photographing anything that may prove to be significant; which usually meant everything.

Once inside, the purpose of the tent became clear. A gap in a chain link fence separated the lane from the drop to the concrete platform under the arch. The damage pointed to regular use, and the lack of an exit on the far side suggested either rough sleepers, or drug addicts frequented the arch; possibly both.

The senior officer noted the fresh opening in the fence at the far end of the tent, closer to the canal; the path to it marked with tape. Creation of the new entry point avoided destruction of any evidence in the original opening.

The two officers stepped through the new gap and dropped eighteen inches to the concrete platform, entering the arch behind the tarpaulin.

SOCO assistants still processed part of the scene, one taking casts of the footprints by the fence, another photographing marks on the wall supporting the railway bridge. Until they finished, the detectives would remain clear of those areas. Close by, another white suited individual knelt beside what at first glance appeared to be a pile of old clothes, abandoned against the brickwork. On closer inspection, the clothes contained a body.

"What we got, Doc?"

"An escalation by the looks of it, Helene."

"Oh bollocks."

Pathologist, Dr James Melbourne turned his head and raised an eyebrow.

"Sorry, James, I just don't need this right now. First the rapes, then these attacks, and now this."

DCI Helene MacKay let out a sigh.

Less than four hundred metres away, the River Thames flowed on its journey to the sea and the unmistakable smell of the tidal mudflats reached her nostrils. Helene shuddered to think what it would have been like in the nineteenth century, with all that sewage flowing into the river.

"Okay, fill me in please, Doc."

"Caucasian male, somewhere between fifty and seventy years old. Hard to tell with rough sleepers. Probably died as a result of blunt force trauma to the body, or possibly the one blow to the head. Lividity would indicate this is probably your murder scene. No signs of the onset of rigor, but at this temperature that could mean a TOD of any time after 10pm. I'll be able to tell you more once we get him back."

The face masks muffled their speech.

"Weapon?"

"You know me by now, Helene. I'm not going to jump to conclusions, but it looks like a broad, round object, such as a baseball bat. Marks on the wall, there, would be consistent with being struck by a bat as they swung."

"Wouldn't surprise me. Ties in with the previous attacks. It was only a matter of time before something like this happened. Well, that will put the growth enhancing product into the air recirculating device won't it?"

A young SOCO assistant frowned.

ONE

"The shit's going to hit the fan." Helene explained. "Thanks, Doc, keep me up to speed."

"And when did I ever not?"

Her eyes crinkled at the corners, the smile hidden beneath the mask.

She turned to her companion.

"Get Uniform to start door-to-door in the flats on both sides of the railway, and the barges over there," Helene said, waving her hand towards the tarpaulin. "Oh, and we better get the underwater unit, just in case they decided to give us a gift and drop the murder weapon in the canal."

"Narrow boats, Ma'am."

"What?"

"Narrow boats. Barges are much wider. Those are narrow boats."

"You'll feel my narrow shoe up your wide arse if you don't get on with it."

DS Barnes' eyes sparkled; presumably he was giving her one of his boyish grins. With only the eyes showing it was hard to tell.

"Yes, Ma'am. On it right away," he said as he stepped out of the tent.

"Bloody youth of today," said Helene, watching Barnes depart.

"You're hardly an old fogey are you? You can't be a day over thirty-five."

"Flattery will get you everywhere, Doc."

The doctor shook his head. "You're too hard on him, Helene."

She shook her head.

"No, not really, he's a good copper. He has the right instincts. Anyway, it never did me any harm."

"You don't think it turned you into a grumpy old

woman then?"

Helene put her hands on her hips.

"What happened to the flattery? Me? Grumpy?" She screwed up her face as if in thought. "Well, maybe until my first coffee, but then I'm all sweetness and light."

"You must tell me sometime where you bought yours?"

She cocked her head to one side.

"Bought my what, James?"

"Rose coloured glasses."

Helene threw her head back and laughed, her breath creating miniature clouds in the cold morning air.

"One day, Doc, you're going to wound me, you know that."

"Yeah, yeah, and one day, you'll buy me the dinner you keep promising me. You know, when I find your evidence for you?"

"Ah but you're a married man, Doc."

"I'm wanting a meal, not your body."

"I live in hope,"

The doctor quickly turned his head, his eyebrows raised, but Helene had already moved away and he watched her as she stepped out of the tent in pursuit of Barnes.

1983

CHAPTER TWO

If fear had a smell, then this place held an abundance of fear. He had known of its existence of course, long before his captors brought him here, but the precise location still remained a mystery to him, and he didn't suppose he would ever know.

Naked and shivering, Harry wasn't sure how much longer he could last. Spread-eagled and leaning against a wall, his muscles burned. He could block the pain; pain was not the problem; it was the uncertainty.

The hood over his head blocked one of his most important senses and dulled another. His captors played clever, a slammed door didn't mean an empty room. That would be too easy.

He could only guess at the time, but the cold water would hit his body long after he thought he was alone. Sometimes it didn't come at all.

His nerves jangled. Of course, that was the idea, keep him on edge and make him crack, give up the information they wanted. He would eventually, everyone did. Others in his group already had, or so they told him; and they did have details only the rest of the group would have. He was

TWO

strong though, he wouldn't crack easily. He would make the bastards work for it.

In his head he ran through scenarios where he would get his revenge; put them in the same situation, see how they liked it. His captors would die a slow and painful death. Those thoughts made it bearable.

Fortunately, they couldn't delve inside his head, deep into the mire, the dark pit of depraved and evil thoughts, the Freudian Id. Not that Harry believed in most of Freud's teachings: It made no sense to him to base an entire theory of the human psyche on the study of neurotic middle-class Viennese women. One part he accepted without question; lurking deep in the recesses of the mind of every single human being, an evil force waited for an opportunity to unleash itself upon the world. For most, deep in the mind is where it would remain, for others, the thoughts would surface, only to be suppressed; for a chosen few, the force would be released and allowed to run its course.

His mind wandered and he recalled his first day at school, a small primary in the heart of industrial Lancashire. A scrawny little kid, his growth spurt yet to come, wide eyes darting everywhere as he entered the school playground holding hands with his mother. One pupil in particular noted his arrival. The resident bully, or 'cock o' the school', mistook Harry's curiosity in his surroundings for a sign of fear. At the morning break, Harry disabused him of the notion he was afraid, in a short but bloody encounter.

To Harry, humans fell into two categories, those in his pack, and those who were not. The ones who were, should not fear him. His devotion to his fellow pack members? Beyond question. And those who weren't, well they didn't matter. They were of no consequence. That wasn't to say they would be forever outside the pack; membership was a fluid affair. After the brief fight, Harry found he had established the first pack of his own.

The rain beat a rhythm on the metal roof of the building, adding syncopation to the white noise playing through the speakers and his thoughts returned to the present. The surrounding noise made little difference to him. Others laughed at his dedication to his yoga, but they wouldn't laugh now. The discipline allowed him to clear his mind of the extraneous sounds, sweep away his earlier thoughts of childhood and concentrate on his plan. Harry found these times relaxing; where he shut out the world and focused within. For some, the time between wakefulness and sleep is a golden time, one in which many problems are solved, but for Harry, the yoga fulfilled the same function.

Free from the intrusion of the outside world he formulated a plan. He now had a trick up his sleeve they would not expect; one-foot wrong, that's all he needed. He didn't care about the consequences. They were not in his pack.

ooOoo

From their vantage point on the other side of the two-way mirror, the two interrogators watched their subject. Here, they could talk without being overheard. Their interrogations followed a set format; set by their superiors, but allowing the interrogators some latitude in the timing of the next 'event'.

"Tough little bastard isn't he?"

"Little?"

"Okay, tough tall bastard then."

"Aye. He'll crack though. Soon I hope."

Captives in this facility were never beaten. The methods here used far more subtle techniques. Constant disorientation, white noise, cold water, pain from the stretched limbs, nakedness, uncertainty, hunger,

TWO

tiredness; all served to break the will.

"He better, I'm hungry."

"You're always bloody hungry. You must have a tapeworm or something."

The soldiers, veterans in the true sense of the word; long term regulars and combat hardened; the ultimate professionals. There was very little they didn't know, and if they didn't, they knew who to call. Even with their wealth of knowledge the learning never stopped; always striving to improve their abilities.

"All that time you spent in the jungle, mate. Bound to catch something nasty. Mind you, not half as worrying as being surrounded by bloody sheep in this god forsaken place."

The two had served together almost from the time they signed up; as familiar with each other as man and wife. Some would say soldiers formed even a stronger bond than matrimony, given their shared experiences.

"You know what they say don't you? When they start to look pretty, it's time to go."

"Funny you should say that. I'm sure I heard a 'baa' coming from your room last night. Was she one of the pretty ones?"

His colleague stuck up two fingers. "Up yours, mate."

Laughing, he patted him on the back. "Let's get back in and finish this."

ooOoo

The voice startled Harry; he must have drifted away.

"Tell us what we want to know. Now!"

He couldn't be sure if they'd recently entered the room or never left in the first place.

He sensed one of his captors change position. Though deprived of sight and his hearing partially muffled from the hood, he still formed a mental picture of the positions of the other soldiers; how accurate, he couldn't tell. When the man changed position he made a rare mistake, moving too close and directly behind Harry; far too close. With all the effort he could muster, Harry kicked one leg back, stretching as high as possible and bringing it behind him to reach the man. Once it made contact he gained enough leverage to lift his other leg into the air. Wrapping both legs around him, Harry pushed away from the wall, twisted his body and reached up to gain a firm grip of the man's neck as they tumbled to the ground. Even though his arms felt numb, and his muscles ached, he exerted as much pressure as he could across the other man's windpipe.

The light startled him, the hood ripped off his head. The second captor held up his hands.

"It's okay, it's okay. You can stop now."

It took Harry a few moments to take in the information. He looked down. He held his tormentor in a headlock; his face turning a strange shade of blue. Harry's body went limp as his muscles relaxed. He released his grip, and listened to the immense gasp as the man took a deep breath. Harry scanned the room, he had not been here before, but he knew where he was. There was no threat to him here.

Strange how the mind played such tricks; the interrogation becoming real to him. It had been real, but only insofar as the training would allow. The 'evade and capture' element being part of his selection to the Special Boat Squadron, the lesser known sister of the SAS. Everyone knew of the SAS and their motto ' Who Dares Wins', typical army bluster and brute force. The SBS were proud of their motto too, 'Not by Strength, by Guile', the thinking man's unit. Well, he showed this SAS sergeant what SBS members are capable of, both in strength and guile, even if he was only on selection. The move he made

TWO

was considered to be impossible and he showed them by applying a little thought to the situation, a way can be found around most obstacles.

"Sergeant Fielding, you'll be taken for debrief now."

A third man entered and threw him some clothes.

"Put those on, then follow me."

CHAPTER THREE

Two officers sat either side of a highly polished mahogany desk. Both held the rank of Major, the one behind the desk being number two I/C of the Special Boat Service, his companion, in charge of one of the four squadrons. Photographs adorned the walls, some of men with blackened faces, others in regimental uniform, and images of high speed RIBs on the sea or men leaping out of inflatables on some unknown shore.

"I'm not sure, Tom. He's a borderline psychopath according to the report, and the two Sergeants say he appeared wild in the interrogation room."

"I know, Bill, and that's why I want him. No one has ever scored so highly on all the other tests, ever. He's almost superhuman and you know it's something I wouldn't say lightly. He's a natural and just what we want for our ops."

Bill shook his head, "He's not stable."

"Is that what the shrink said?"

"Well not exactly, but..."

THREE

"There you go then. We need people like him, people on the edge. Be honest, with your back to the wall who would you rather have on your side, someone like him, or someone who plays by the rules?"

Bill rose from his desk and stood by the window overlooking Hamworthy Camp, the SBS headquarters in Poole, Dorset. The trees around the car park swayed in the almost gale force winds; the rain lashing against the window like a demented car wash. Somewhere in that awful weather one of the squadrons was on a navigation exercise. Good luck to them.

"Look, I understand what you're saying but what about those other times. Would you feel safe around him?"

"His loyalty is already without question. He's demonstrated that on more than one occasion. You saw his Falklands reports. The man looks after his own even when doing so puts himself in danger and on the selection he proved to be an excellent team player."

Bill continued to stare out of the window, the silence broken only by the ticking of a clock and the rain lashing against the pane.

"I think we should RTU him."

"There's nothing on his record to indicate a problem. We need people like him, ruthless, calculating but disciplined. He has an exemplary record. He came through basic and jungle without any issues. The question of his mental state only arose when he tackled the SAS interrogator, and frankly from what I've seen he deserved what he got. Got a little bit too cocky and a step too close. Have you ever seen anyone else pull a stunt like that? It shouldn't be possible, that's why we put them in that position. You can't do anything leaning against a wall. He did. He's resourceful and dangerous and that is who I would rather have alongside me. I promise if any more doubts are raised during SC training, I'll RTU him."

"Oh, he's dangerous all right, and that concerns me." Bill sighed and shook his head slowly before coming to a decision.

"Okay Tom, but if this goes wrong I can't protect you. You know my feelings."

"Thanks, Bill. It'll be fine. I'm certain."

"You better be. Your career's on the line."

ND**1991**

CHAPTER FOUR

The submarine wallowed in the slight swell, the blue painted camouflage pattern hastily added in Diego Garcia, already peeling away. The shallow waters of the Arabian Gulf necessitated breaking up the outline of the submarine, making her harder to spot from the air. Water smacked against the hull, the sound reminded Harry of the fish being slapped onto slabs by the busy fishmongers in Rochdale Market; memories of childhood drifted in at the strangest of moments.

Some lookouts scanned the horizon for other boats or enemy aircraft, others scanned the waters around the hull; the submarine lay in an area suspected to have been mined by the Iraqis. The water depth here was less than ten metres in places, giving HMS Opossum little room to manoeuvre, and the enemy occupied territory close by. No wonder Captain Upright appeared nervous as he looked down from the bridge.

The squadron worked quietly in the dark readying the

FOUR

Zodiac and they soon pulled away from the submarine towards the shoreline, some sixteen kilometres away. They planned to use the outboard motor on the first part of the journey, then switch to paddles for the final approach to the beach.

Harry could hear the fizz and hiss as the waves ebbed and flowed on the sandy shoreline. They must be close now. Reconnaissance photographs showed the Iraqis installing defences along the beach. The latest intelligence suggested this area remained still unprotected. He hoped so. He didn't fancy having to work his way through barbed wire, and the inevitable mine field.

He wore a dirty and ragged dishdasha beneath his black dry suit. He found it uncomfortable, but he couldn't risk wearing anything light in the boat. He would be too visible, and anyway, he would need to wade ashore. The black waterproof bag slung over his shoulder contained an equally scruffy gahfiya, gutra and ogal, the traditional headwear. He had not shaved or washed for two weeks. Other members of the team kept their distance, something they had trouble doing on board the cramped submarine.

At six feet tall he cut a distinguished figure, but adopting a stooping posture made him appear smaller and frail. The dishdasha would hide his well-honed physique. He must convince locals and Iraqis alike to ignore him; blend into the background, as most beggars did.

Damn. The intel was wrong. Razor wire stretched across the sand. For two kilometres they worked the boat along the shore, away from Kuwait City, before they found the end of the wire.

One man scanned the land with night vision binoculars. They didn't want any nasty surprises. He signalled the all clear to the team. It didn't matter how many times he did this, Harry always got a shot of adrenalin when a mission was signalled 'go'.

As they silently paddled the dinghy in to the shore, Harry continued his mental preparations. He thought in

Arabic. From now on he must only speak and think in Arabic, there could be no mistakes. A word out of place would cost him his life.

A peaceful solution was still being sought by the UN, but it was apparent to everyone involved, the Iraqis did not intend to withdraw. The C in C thought it better to get people on the ground before hostilities commenced.

Still a few metres from the land, Harry and two others dropped into the surprisingly cold water and waded ashore. Once safely on the beach, the two men took up defensive positions while Harry removed his dry suit. He retrieved his ogal from the waterproof bag and made a final check of the remaining contents; rat packs, water, purification tablets, satellite radio and Glock P7; his F-S knife contained in a sheath inside the left sleeve of his dishdasha.

"Il'l-liqa." *Until we meet again*.

"Insh'Allah," Harry replied. *If god wills*.

Harry moved up the beach keeping low. Houses dotted the area, but more importantly there would be troops stationed here. The Iraqis may not have started the shore defences on this stretch, but it would almost certainly be patrolled; they were on high alert for a seaborne invasion. The Zodiac would lay off for ten minutes then, if all was well, return to rendezvous with the submarine, which had moved further out to sea and submerged to periscope depth to await a signal from the returning party.

Harry flashed an 'all clear' in the direction of the Zodiac and moved closer to the road. He would have to cover forty kilometres to reach the city. As they landed shortly after midnight, rather than risk moving now, he would find somewhere to hole up until tomorrow night. No sense in taking chances and getting caught. He harboured no illusions what would happen to him if the Iraqis found him carrying military equipment. He crossed the road, putting some distance between himself and the

FOUR

beach, then searched for a suitable place to lay up for the day.

ooOoo

Kuwait City was a mess. Most of the shops had been looted; furniture piled up outside villas and apartments. This was not a highly trained occupation force: it was a rabble. He heaved a sigh of relief. No one knew for certain what to expect, but of all the scenarios, this was the least expected and the most welcome. A cohesive fighting force would be harder to evade. The troops here proved to be slack and lazy, and these were supposed to be the best. That wasn't to say they weren't dangerous. The lack of discipline could result in his death, purely because someone didn't like his face. On the other hand, it would allow him more freedom than he first thought.

It took two nights of ducking and diving before he finally arrived in the heart of the city. He needed to find somewhere safe to stash the equipment and set up a base. He knew there was a resistance movement here, but would avoid them. No one could know who he was, or what he was doing. He couldn't take the risk of someone giving him away to the Iraqis.

Getting here had been the easy part, passing through the relatively sparsely populated suburbs. Moving around the city after curfew was decidedly dodgy, but until he found somewhere to hide the bag he couldn't chance moving during the day. Finally, he found what he was looking for in the form of a looted shop, clearly abandoned, the door hanging off the bottom hinge.

Strewn around outside lay what he assumed to be some of the fittings from the shop, shelving and display racks, Paper flapped and fluttered in the breeze, adding to the air of desolation. Kuwait had been violated. This was no invasion with the sole intention of annexing the country. This was a deliberate attempt to destroy its very existence.

HARRY

Harry checked the immediate area for escape routes. Plenty of narrow alleyways to disappear into, and neighbouring buildings close enough for him to escape across the rooftops if necessary. He would do his utmost to make sure it wasn't necessary, but he couldn't control the actions of others. He checked the back of the shop; no exit there, both a blessing and a curse. His only way out would be over the rooftops if anyone came in, but neither could he be surprised from behind. To the front was open ground, affording him a good view of someone approaching from that direction.

Time to hunker down and get some sleep, but first he needed food and water. The journey from the beach had been a short one by SBS standards, but nerve-racking nonetheless. It was much easier to work as a team, than work alone behind enemy lines. Finding this shop was a good piece of luck. He had shelter and water readily available and enough rations to keep him going for some time. Of course, as a beggar he hoped to be able to supplement the rat-packs, at least with a bit of fruit if nothing else. The packs were okay as far as they went, but after a while they could become monotonous.

Upstairs he found a single room over the shop. A few pictures still adorned the walls. Clearly the soldiers who had looted this place did not have any interest in art. Broken glass from the window littered the bare floorboards, and plaster dust covered what bits of furniture remained. Until recently, this had been someone's home, and now it would be his for the foreseeable future. He kicked away the broken glass from in front of the window, sat on the floor leaning his back against the wall, and settled down for what remained of the night. He broke out a rat-pack and set about feeding himself. Tomorrow, the difficult work would start.

ooOoo

FOUR

There it was again. It wasn't his imagination. Something moved in the shop below. No need to be alarmed yet, it may be a dog. Okay, maybe not, not unless dogs had learned to open drawers. Someone was searching the shop. For several minutes he listened as the person rummaged through the debris, no doubt looking for anything of value that had been overlooked.

The sounds stopped, then Harry heard the one thing he didn't want to hear, boots on the staircase.

He eased himself off the floor, taking care not to make a sound. Not that it would matter, the person coming up the stairs clearly thought the building was unoccupied, and was making enough noise to mask anything that Harry did.

He positioned himself behind the half-open door. In his hands he held a piece of piano wire, the ends of which were wrapped around two small wooden toggles. He had never used the garrotte in anger, but he certainly knew how. Unless the intruder changed his mind, Harry was about to make his first hand-to-hand kill.

An Iraqi soldier stepped into the room, his senses remained heightened even though he was intent on finding something to loot. As Harry stepped out behind him, the soldier started to turn. It was too late. The wire bit into his neck, slicing deep into the skin as Harry pulled it tight.

Dropping his weapon on the wooden floor, the soldier frantically clawed at wire. Harry stepped slowly backwards, the enemy desperately trying to step with him. By pulling the soldier towards him, Harry kept the man off balance, not giving him the opportunity to counterattack. Pulling him closer, Harry craned his neck round to see into the soldier's face. He saw the fear give way to acceptance as the man realised he was about to die. The garrotte cut off the blood supply to the brain and the soldier passed out. Harry kept the pressure on the neck until he heard the last agonal gasp leave the man's body.

HARRY

Harry knew he should feel sick. He had taken another man's life, at close quarter. He should be justifying it as self-defence, as a necessary part of war. Kill or be killed.

To his surprise, he found he didn't feel that way. He felt elated, euphoric even. The adrenaline flowed freely, and he loved it. This is what had been missing from his life. It was the most exciting thing ever to happen to him.

Although he served in the Falklands War, survived the Sir Galahad, and had been in combat, he never killed anyone at close quarters. He shot people, at a distance, saw others close to him die, but he had never taken a life with his own hands. It gave him a sense of fulfilment he never thought he would achieve. Holding the balance of power over someone's life in like that was the ultimate control. He had never tried any drugs in his life but he could imagine this would better any high they could give; the ultimate addiction.

Harry lowered the body to the floor and searched the dead man for items of value, not monetary value, but survival value. The most obvious being the soldier's AK-47, but he couldn't carry that around with him. He would have to stash it somewhere safe, to be used as a last resort. Judging from the uniform, this man was likely a conscript, certainly not one of the infamous Republican Guard. From the briefings Harry received, he understood the Iraqi forces remained under-resourced and underfed, creating a situation where the soldiers resorted to looting to survive. That, and greed of course; a sign of an undisciplined army. Nevertheless, they carried weapons, and that made them dangerous, and had to be treated with respect.

The sound of more boots on rubble caused Harry to freeze. Someone else moved in the shop downstairs. Perhaps he heard the gun fall to the floor.

"Hakim? Hakim, ayn 'ant?" *Where are you?*

Harry looked around. He couldn't move the body: the man downstairs would hear him. Fortunately, the dead

FOUR

man lay out of sight of the doorway. The soldier coming now wouldn't be a pushover like the last one. He was wary; his companion not answering. His nerves would be jangling, making him jumpy and unpredictable.

Harry moved cautiously and quietly, once again taking up position behind the door, but this time he crouched. He doubted he would be able to use the garrotte on this occasion. He reached for the F-S knife concealed in his sleeve. This would have to be done the hard way.

The soldier placed each foot with care, slowly edging his way into the room. Harry remained motionless. Sweat ran down his brow, dripping into his eyes, but he dare not move a muscle. Only a couple of inches of wood separated him from his enemy. In other circumstances, a round fired through the door would be the solution, but not here. He had no idea how many other troops might be within earshot. Something moved beyond the edge of the door. The man's shoulder came into view. Unbelievably, he had his back to Harry. This soldier was not well-trained. He had placed himself in a vulnerable position with his back to the door, one which would cost him his life.

Before the man had time to react, Harry leapt up, grabbing the man's head with one hand and plunging the knife into the side of his neck with the other. In a swift movement he sliced forward, out of the soldier's throat, severing the carotid arteries and windpipe. The soldier couldn't utter a sound and with the blood supply cut off to his brain, in a matter of seconds he lost consciousness. Harry pushed the dying man away from him. He couldn't look into his face this time, there was too much blood pumping from the wound. He couldn't get covered in that. Two kills in a matter of minutes.

He was singing inside. This is what he had been trained for, but little did they know when they trained him, this was what he longed for. Hell, he hadn't known it himself.

CHAPTER FIVE

All throughout his childhood, Nicky Rolands longed to move away from the East End. He wanted to be somebody, a leading politician - Prime Minister even. He got his chance when he won a place at Glasgow University to study politics. Once there, he found politics bored him immensely, and while finishing his degree he drifted into journalism after landing a job as a reporter for the Glasgow University Guardian newspaper.

Now, after a near death experience the previous year, he found himself back in London and across the street from the Central Criminal Court, otherwise known as The Old Bailey. The magnificent sculpture of Lady Justice looked out across London, sword in one hand and scales in the other; unlike many of her counterparts around the world, this lady did not wear a blindfold, her maidenly form guaranteeing her impartiality. He crossed the street and entered the building through the impressive public entrance and was soon directed to one of the several witness rooms. The marble corridors imparted an air of tradition and seriousness about the place, which indeed

FIVE

was the case. He was about to give evidence in one of the most famous courts in the world, Court Number One. Dr Crippen, Peter Sutcliffe - the Yorkshire Ripper, and the last woman to be executed in the United Kingdom, Ruth Ellis, all stood trial here, and Nicky was going to be a part of another piece of history. If justice prevailed, Munro would be going away for a long time, but if he got off, Nicky would need to find somewhere to hide; the moon might be just far enough.

Although he was in awe of his surroundings, it was nothing compared to the prospect of facing Munro again; one of London's most notorious gangsters, one who managed to evade prosecution for nigh on thirty years, one who, according to rumours, hearsay and local folklore, had ordered many a person to 'disappear' in the waters of the River Thames; Nicky was almost one of them.

No stranger to courtrooms, having covered a number of cases in Aberdeen when he wrote for a local paper, the Press and Journal, Nicky was surprised to see his hands trembling uncontrollably. He must calm himself before giving evidence. Observing and testifying were two vastly different experiences.

As the date of the case approached he suffered recurring nightmares, standing in the witness box, his mouth moving but unable to make a sound. What if it came true; what if he couldn't speak?

The past few months had been a rollercoaster ride for him. While visiting Inverness Airport, he spotted an old school friend; someone unlikely to have business in that part of the world. On a hunch Nicky stayed out of sight and followed him. His instincts proved spot on and the hunch paid off, as he witnessed a failed attempt at a robbery. His pal had somehow been involved in the incident and knowing he now worked for Donald Munro, Nicky travelled south to London to see what he could unearth. Unfortunately, one of Munro's henchmen caught him snooping around outside Munro's offices, resulting in him being manhandled inside for a 'chat' with the man himself.

He heard his name being called, interrupting his thoughts and bringing him back to the present. He crossed the Grand Hall and had but a moment to take in the rich decor of this splendid architecture, mirroring the dome of the nearby St Paul's Cathedral. He was ushered into the court room, to be once again in the presence of Munro.

The accused never took his eyes off Nicky for one moment. Rather than being intimidated, Nicky gained a new strength from the stare and found himself giving evidence calmly and assuredly. Over the next hour he gave a clear account of the incident. Not once did his voice falter, even under cross-examination. After testifying, the Judge excused him from the stand and allowed him to sit in the court to watch the rest of the proceedings. To his disappointment, his testimony for the prosecution was the last to be heard, and the court adjourned until the next day.

The case for the defence rested on the fact Munro had not been present when his men took Nicky aboard the fishing vessel, and was not party to the actions of the men on board. To a man, Munro's men testified their boss played no part in their actions that day, and they had taken matters into their own hands. Nicky watched the faces of the jury while this evidence was being given, and if he'd been a gambling man he would have laid odds that not one member of the jury believed it for a single moment.

In the summing up, he struggled not to laugh out loud when the defence counsel painted Munro as a pillar of the community, citing his long list of charitable acts and suggesting Munro had been the victim of overzealous employees.

The Judge presented a brief summary to the jury and

FIVE

they retired to consider their verdict. No one expected them to return just forty-five minutes later, but return they did, and delivered their verdict of 'guilty' to the charge of 'conspiracy to murder.'

The Judge adjourned the court for sentencing but not before Munro addressed Nicky.

"I'll hunt you down, Rolands. Mark my words."

A finger stabbed the air impaling each word in its venomous fury.

Munro was still yelling at Nicky as he was manhandled out of the dock to the cells below.

Nicky watched him being taken away and felt nothing. No anger, no fear, no hatred; the man tried to kill him, and now he would pay for it. Munro's associates had already been tried, convicted, sentenced and faced a long stretch in prison. The calmness felt at the beginning of his evidence remained. The world held no fear for him anymore.

Outside the court a group of reporters waited to interview him, but he gave nothing away. Why would he? He was a journalist, and this was an opportunity to write his own piece.

As he made his way from the throng, a voice rang out.

"Nicky 'bloody' Rolands."

He turned to see a familiar figure striding towards him, DCI MacIntyre, the Grampian Police detective leading the investigation into the theft of a helicopter.

"What brings you here, Detective?"

"The chance to see that scrote go down. Well done, lad. I know I've given you a hard time over the years, but that was a solid piece of work from you there."

Nicky was taken aback. MacIntyre never allowed him near a case he was running, was uncooperative and uncommunicative, and now here he was giving him a compliment.

The detective offered his hand and Nicky shook it.

"Just don't take this as a sign I'm going soft. Anyhow, I'm retiring soon so you won't have to worry about me anymore."

The detective patted him on the back, shook his hand once more and turned to leave.

"When you get back to Aberdeen, lad, you can buy me a pint."

A short, well-dressed man hovered nearby. As MacIntyre left, he approached Nicky.

"Mr Rolands, I know you will want to write your own piece on the trial and the events leading up to it, so call in to my offices tomorrow and we'll see what can be arranged."

He handed Nicky a business card, and with that he was gone.

Nicky turned the card over in his hand. 'Sir David English.'

His jaw dropped. If he was not mistaken, one of the finest journalists in the land, and longstanding editor of the Daily Mail, had just invited him to come and write a piece for his paper.

Well, well, well. It looks like I could be in Fleet Street after all, he thought, smiling.

2016

CHAPTER SIX

As far back as he could remember, Andrew Leslie hated blacks, browns, yellows, and any other race you could possibly imagine. And as for religious groups, he couldn't think of a single one he would tolerate. In truth, if you weren't a white Anglo-Saxon you found yourself on his hate list. Ironically, he was an Australian by birth, a fact that seemed to have passed him by completely.

He hated everyone so much, he felt it was his duty to educate the world on the subject of white British supremacy. He was unaware the world in general was far more educated than he. As part of his plan he formed a neo-Nazi group, Britain Against Racial Equality, BARE. He was fond of promoting the BARE facts about the various ethnic groups and religions, none of which would be considered a fact by anyone who had the ability to think for themselves. Which is why he had only a small but vociferous following of under-educated like-minded non-thinkers.

Leslie believed by ridding the world of these 'parasites', as he liked to think of them, it would become a sort of utopia; free of disease, war and crime. To any

SIX

sane person it was glaringly obvious he was as much a part of the problem as the people he hated. When not racially abusing or beating someone, he would either be out of his mind on drugs, or dealing on a street corner. Jobs never lasted more than a few days before his extreme views and violent temper got him dismissed, or he left of his own volition. In short, he was a good-for-nothing bully and a walking stereotype. Of course, he didn't think of himself that way. A free thinker, a leader, a visionary, the history books would show him to be all of these things, of that he was certain. But for now, the world didn't understand him, it didn't understand the need to remove the human vermin and make the planet a much better place.

The skunk was good; he was feeling chilled. He lay on his sofa, dreaming of the day the world would be free, and he would be acknowledged as the saviour of the human race. His thoughts turned to the recent attacks on the homeless. How dare they? These people were not scum. A lot were solid British stock, some even served their country in the military, fighting the very people he was fighting, as he saw it. Their predicament had been thrust upon them by immigrants and non-whites. If it wasn't for them they would all be in employment with a roof over their heads. They should be helped, not beaten. If only he could get his hands on the toe-rags that were doing this. He would stake his next score on the fact the attacks were being done by blacks or Asians.

He knew what his next move should be. He would get the rest of BARE together and they would keep watch on as many of the rough sleeping places as they could. He didn't like the crusties too much either, but he would rather protect them than see some 'ethnic minority', as they liked to be known, get away with these attacks.

Ethnic minority? My arse, he thought. Not the words he would use for them at all.

CHAPTER SEVEN

The Old Man shuffled his feet as he walked. He was a tall figure once, but now he stooped forward, almost as though his head wanted to arrive first. His matted hair escaped from under a dirty trilby hat. The old brown mac had seen better days; torn and tatty, with reminders of long forgotten food and drink scattered down the front, like shadows on a wall. Grey trousers continued the theme; patched and stained, two sizes too big, though perhaps they once fitted his now bony frame; the only defiance to gravity was the twine wrapped around his waist. His shoes were dusty and the soles flapped like a pair of silent mouths. As he shuffled he mumbled through the ragged beard which competed with his hair to hide the leathery face, his eyes shaded by the grey verandas of eyebrows.

No one so much as glanced at him. Passers-by always found something more interesting to warrant their attention. He was one of the invisible people whose existence most of society preferred not to acknowledge. It wasn't easy to look at others less fortunate than yourself.

SEVEN

You might have to face up to the shortcomings of a system which allowed people to end up this way. No one liked to be reminded of that. The Old Man cared little though.

As was the case with some of the others on the streets, he once wore a uniform with pride; his green beret still his most prized possession. He missed the camaraderie, the shared fears and successes, the sense of belonging. Where had it all gone? If anyone came near him long enough, and if he deigned them worthy of his time, he would tell them where it all went, bloody defence cuts that's where. Every few years one government or another would decide to cut the size of the armed forces, it didn't matter which party, they were all the damned same. He was in the wrong place at the wrong time, just the right age, and bang, out on his ear. 'Thank you for risking your life for us all these years, here's your resettlement package, off you go, there's a good chap, don't spend it all at once.' And that was that.

He did not take to civilian life, it lacked discipline; a sense of belonging. And it didn't have much call for people who excelled at hiding themselves and killing others. In the early years of being in Civvy Street, he made hundreds of job applications, and for his efforts he received a handful of replies and even fewer interviews. All ended the same way; 'Sorry, you are not quite what we are looking for.' Gradually the applications dwindled along with his interest, and eventually he gave up. Now, he had no possibility of getting a job. Screw them all, he thought, they weren't worthy of my time anyway.

Finally, he found the camaraderie he craved on the streets and in the parks; not quite the same as the brotherhood he left behind in the forces, but still, they were a good bunch and in the main they looked after each other. They had their ups and downs, but didn't any family? And they were family to him, his only family; he no longer had any blood relatives. They thought of themselves that way; family members. During the day small groups would congregate in a park or by the waterways, anywhere they could sit and talk, reminisce, or even just share a silent moment together. At night, some would gather together to sleep in close proximity, especially by the river, while others would find somewhere secluded for the night and sleep alone.

These were the people who fell through the gaps; the ones for whom the system could not cater. For some, it was self-inflicted, unwilling to abide by the rules, while for others, Lady Luck had turned her back on them and through no fault of their own they found themselves without a roof over their heads. Yet all were judged the same by many of those fortunate enough to not be in the same situation. Some understood the plight of these people but they were in a minority. At one time the Old Man would have been a judge too. It never crossed his mind that not all the homeless were there from their own making. He knew that now. Hindsight was a wonderful teacher and the streets a great leveller. What you once were didn't count here. There was only the here and now.

A change fell on the streets in recent weeks. Attacks on a few of the lone sleepers had cast a shadow over the whole group. Confirmed night soloists now joined the larger bands. Safety can always be found in numbers and until these bastards were caught it made no sense to be isolated. The Old Man raged inside. Why would anyone want to hurt these people? What harm did they do to anyone?

CHAPTER EIGHT

The officers of the MIT gathered around the table for the morning briefing. A white board mounted on the wall contained a list of the major facts of the case. A red pin on the map denoted the location of the murder, and a scattering of blue pins, where the attacks had taken place. The identity of the deceased had been tentatively established as Brian Hamilton, a former Falklands veteran. Helene opened the proceedings.

"The victim died of positional asphyxiation, not blunt force trauma. This suggests the blow to the head rendered him unconscious and his chin down position against the wall blocked his airway. Not the COD we expected"

There was a groan from one of the officers. Helene continued.

"Yep, you've seen it Mike. Depending on how it's played the perpetrators might get away on a manslaughter charge. But at the moment we gather the evidence and nick the bastards who did it. After that, the wigs can argue over the finer points of law.

"Sickening though isn't it Ma'am, to think they can go

EIGHT

around smacking people about, and when someone dies the law protects them, or at the very least gives them a way out?"

Helene nodded her agreement.

"It's frustrating, although I'm not sure manslaughter charges are really a way out, but our job is to enforce the law. It's up to others to decide how they are used. Okay, Adam, what have we from forensics?

Detective Inspector Adam Renton got to his feet.

"A baseball or cricket bat is suspected to be the weapon. From the parallel or railway-track bruising on the body, the baseball bat is almost certainly a favourite. SOCO found particles of wood in the marks on the wall where it's believed the bat struck during the attack. Hairs found on the victim are away for DNA analysis. Shoe prints obtained from the area around the fence matched a partial on the victim. A second set, Forensics believe are contemporaneous with the first, suggesting two persons carried out the attack. A search of the National Footprint Database tells us we are looking for Nike Air Huarache and Air Tech Challenge III training shoes."

Set up in 2007, the database contained thousands of patterns of shoe prints from the world's shoe manufacturers. It enabled officers to be on the lookout for the correct type of footwear when investigating a crime, and had proved invaluable in several high profile cases.

"Something to bear in mind when interviewing suspects when we get to that stage. Anything else, Adam?"

Renton shook his head.

"Has house-to-house turned up anything?"

DS Barnes also shook his head.

"No Ma'am. A few of the narrow-boat residents commented on the fact the homeless slept there often, but no one saw or heard anything unusual that night."

Helene noted his emphasis on 'narrow-boat' and a brief twitch of a smile touched her lips. He was a cheeky bugger, but he got away with it because he was good. The same could be said for all of her team, she only took the best. Her high clear-up rate was not an accident. They knew what was expected of them, and they delivered. In return, she gave them credit for the work and her full support, unlike some other officers she could name. She turned to the two detectives tasked with re-reading the notes about the previous attacks on the homeless.

"Mary, Deepak, anything in the files?"

"Precious little Ma'am," answered Mary. "All the attacks occurred at the weekend, Friday or Saturday night and, as far as we can tell, in the early hours. Most of the homeless don't have watches, but one of the injured was spotted by a taxi driver. That attack had just occurred and the taxi driver noted the time to be 3.20am."

Helen closed her eyes for a few moments, before speaking.

"So this is the first to occur on a weekday. Perhaps whoever did this isn't responsible for the other attacks. My gut tells me they are linked, but we need to keep an open mind. We may have two groups on the go. The attacks occurring at the weekend suggests to me the perpetrators are employed. So why would they switch to a weekday?"

DS Barnes idly twiddled his pencil in his fingers.

"They had a day off? They know when to strike and how to move around without being seen. Most attacks took place near the canals. Perhaps they live on one of the narrow-boats, Ma'am."

"Possibly, but a lot of homeless choose to sleep near the canals. Less likelihood of being disturbed.

DS Barnes pursed his lips and nodded his head in acknowledgment.

EIGHT

"The idea of a day off isn't a bad one, Davey, but there must be hundreds of folk in the area had a day off yesterday."

Helene looked at the incident board and the map. The canals may be a vital part of the case, on the other hand the southern part of the district was bisected and bordered by canals and rivers, including the Thames. It would be hard not to be near water. She yawned. Too many late nights and not enough sleep. Some self-inflicted and others not. God, she could do without this. She needed a holiday.

CHAPTER NINE

"Rolands, get your arse out of that chair and see what you can find out about these attacks that are happening on the down and outs."

Nicky rolled his eyes. Not once, when he'd been editor-in-chief, did he ever speak to his staff like that, and especially not his more senior staff, nor did he ever bypass the chain of command. How do the managing-editors feel when he comes striding out of his office, barking orders, ignoring any of their planning? This whippersnapper has an arrogance beyond belief, perhaps it was something to do with the fact the owner of the newspaper was his uncle. It certainly didn't appear to be anything to do with his management abilities, which at best were mixed.

After the court case with Munro, Nicky's uncanny ability to get the inside story was soon discovered by Fleet Street, as it was still referred to, even though by the time Nicky got there the majority of the papers were dispersed around the city and no longer located in that iconic landmark of the British press. The invitation to write his story for The Daily Mail led to him remaining there as a

NINE

staff member, eventually, rising to the position of editor-in-chief. At the start of his journalistic career, the position of editor-in-chief of a national newspaper was Nicky's dream position. However, in true Nicky style, once he attained that dream, he found he didn't want it at all. He missed the thrill of uncovering someone's darkest little secret, following up on leads until a story worthy of the front pages emerged. Nicky was a hands on person, and a damned good one at that. He cut his newspaper teeth on investigative journalism in Glasgow, and continued in Aberdeen, so being confined to an office, attending innumerable meetings, and dealing with staff issues bored him almost as much as the politics he studied at University.

He gritted his teeth, kept his head down and got on with it for several years until his loathing of the routine got the better of him. After a long discussion with the owner, he resigned his position and returned to the newsroom as a senior reporter. That was when this snotty-nosed kid, who had all the right connections, stepped in and became top-dog. Perhaps he was being a little unfair, the kid possessed some good skills; managing people however, wasn't one of them.

The true irony of all this was Nicky found himself back in the area where as a child he longed to leave, London's East End. Just a stone's throw from where he grew up.

"That's Mr Rolands to you...sir." He smiled sweetly at his boss, who acknowledged him with a scowl.

"Just bloody get on with it."

Nicky sighed and imperceptibly shook his head while resisting the temptation to give him the finger. Although he and the owner went back a long way, he wasn't related, and blood is thicker than water, as they say. He would not push things too far. Besides, the story would get him out of the office for a while.

HARRY

He grabbed his jacket off the chair and said, "Yes, sir. Of course, sir," and just loud enough for his colleagues to hear. "Three bags full, sir."

The young editor-in-chief turned and strode back towards his office and Nicky gave into the temptation of the single digit, which brought a couple of stifled laughs from around him.

Even with the hustle and bustle of a busy newsroom he somehow heard the sniggers and swung round to see where they were coming from; a moment sooner and he would have caught Nicky's gesture. Instead he saw Nicky raise a finger in a universal sign of 'please wait I have a question.'

"It might help if you told me where these attacks have taken place, London's a mighty big place you know." Nicky gave him another smile.

The editor scowled once more.

Nicky thought back to his childhood and being told if he pulled a face and the wind changed, it would stay that way forever. He wondered if grandmothers still said that to their grandkids.

"Do I have to do all of your work for you, Rolands? Tower Hamlets, you cretin."

Nicky smiled sweetly once more.

"On it, boss."

The editor hated being called boss almost as much as he hated Nicky smiling. Nicky suspected putting both together must drive him up the wall. Oh dear, what a shame.

Had he been a vindictive sort of person he would start to plot his revenge, but he couldn't hold a grudge, well, not for long anyway. And to be frank, this young lad didn't warrant the effort. He just wished he would realise Nicky gave up his position as editor, with a view to going back to the investigative work, the Pulitzer Prize kind, not

NINE

covering stories any youngster just out of journalism school could handle with ease. Nicky was one of the best investigative journalists in the land and this man couldn't seem to grasp the fact. What would it take to convince him otherwise?

Perhaps it was time to move on. To do what though? He was fifty-one for heaven's sake. What could he do at that age apart from journalism? No, he would stick to what he knew best until he retired, then maybe he would keep his hand in by writing newsletters for some charity or something. At least retiring early was a possibility. He had enough put away for that and a private pension he could take early; being single meant he could do pretty much as he liked.

He came back to the task in hand. The boss said the attacks took place in the Tower Hamlets district. A place Nicky knew well, he should do, not only was he born there, but when he took the editor's position, he bought an apartment there.

As would be expected of any journalist worth his salt, he made many contacts throughout London and further afield. He had an idea where to start for this story. Someone who knew the streets first-hand.

He would track down the Old Man, that shouldn't be too difficult. Nicky knew all his favourite haunts.

CHAPTER TEN

Nicky hoped the Old Man would be here. Sometimes a conversation with him was just what he needed to ground him, and to see the world from another perspective. This visit would be both business and pleasure.

He first came across the Old Man when doing a piece about London's homeless a number of years earlier. Over the years their chats became more regular. It took a long time for the old boy to open up to him. He warmed to Nicky when he realised he had a genuine interest in his plight and wasn't just another one of those middle-class do-gooders who liked to help as long as they didn't actually have to go near anyone from the streets. After all these years Nicky considered him to be a true friend and not merely an acquaintance. This friendship, like all true friendships, was based on a genuine warmth to each other, not on the possible benefits that knowing the other person might bring.

Nicky's boss wanted him to do a piece on the attacks, and so he would, but almost certainly not in the way his boss expected. Nicky would do this properly, unlike his boss whose approach would be to have Nicky rehash a

TEN

previously released piece, then move him on to skim over some other story in the same manner. That's why the paper was going down the tubes. None of their stories had any human interest in them. There was no depth, no feeling involved with them; and that was not Nicky's style.

From his early days of investigative journalism for the Glasgow University Guardian, through his time with the Press & Journal in Aberdeen, and to his current role on Fleet Street, Nicky always looked for the human angle. And that's what his boss would get now, whether he liked it or not.

Bow Road was the Old Man's usual stomping ground, though not his only place. He sometimes liked to sleep near one of the canals or in Tower Hamlets Cemetery Park, and occasionally he would still try to find somewhere near the Olympic Stadium in Stratford. Not that there were many places to sleep around there now. As the Olympics approached, the homeless found themselves being shut out of the area around the Olympic Park. This Nicky learned from the Old Man and he suspected it had been part of a sanitisation package designed to make the world think there were no social problems in the UK; how very Nineteen Eighty-Four. Even before the Olympics, Bow Road and in particular the church of St Mary-atte-Bow were amongst the Old Man's favourite haunts.

Nicky found him in his usual place, on the bench nearest to the main entrance of the church. Although the Old Man wandered a lot, he was still a creature of habit, choosing the same bench or corner whenever he visited a particular place. Nicky plonked himself down beside the Old Man who stopped his mumbling for a moment before turning to take a look at the interloper.

"Oh it's you."

Nicky handed him a coffee. The Old Man screwed his face up at the name on the paper cup but nodded his thanks and took a sip before pulling another face.

"Where's the sugar?"

"Sorry."

It was one of those rare, frosty, crisp, sunny mornings, that Mother Nature occasionally brought forth to tease a winter London; a hint of a summer that would inevitably fail to materialise. A blackbird competed with the traffic on the main road, its song a delightful contrast to the constant commotion of the busy thoroughfare.

Nicky spoke first.

"I suppose you've heard?"

"Oh aye, lad. It's a permanent feature of living on the streets, but it's more than that now isn't it?"

"Yes, you told me once before, but this is different isn't it? More...well...organised, I suppose."

The Old Man nodded.

"It seems personal somehow. Sometimes, someone gets beaten and their boots taken, or food they have hidden, but this seems to be because they are living rough. With these attacks nothing ever gets taken. Least, that's what I hear. Old Tommy Two Teeth reckons it's kids, having a bit of a laugh. No laughing matter now is it? Let 'em try it with me, that's what I say."

He was clearly agitated. These were his friends, most of them anyway. There were only one or two he wouldn't give the time of day to.

"Has anyone seen anything?"

The Old Man pulled a face and shook his head.

"Nah. They seem to strike in the early hours when there's no one around. Least that's what I've heard. Only go for the loners, never where there are a few of us."

"You're a loner. Doesn't it worry you that something might happen? If they aren't careful someone could die."

TEN

The Old Man turned to him, his bloodshot eyes searching Nicky's face.

"You don't know, do you?"

Nicky looked at him in puzzlement.

"Know what?"

The Old Man exhaled slowly, trying to keep it all together. He closed his eyes and rested his face on the fist of his left hand. For a few moments he sat motionless, then threw his head back and took in a large gasp of air.

His eyes locked with Nicky's.

"They found a body this morning. I reckon it's Brian Hamilton. His kipping place anyhow."

Nicky felt a chill go through him. He brushed back his hair with both hands and then clasped them at the back of his head. This was not what he had been expecting to hear.

"Oh jeez, I'm sorry...I..." Nicky wasn't sure what to say, finally settling on, "I was asked to find out what I could about the attacks, I didn't know about Brian. I'm...I'm shocked. I'm so sorry."

The Old Man leaned forward, rested his elbows on his knees, put his head in his hands and started to rock gently back and forth.

"Now't for you to be sorry about, lad. Unless you did it that is, and you don't strike me as the sort who'd wish harm on anyone. I don't suppose the news is out yet, but word gets around on the street pretty quick. I just assumed that's why you were here."

The spell of sunshine proved to be short lived and vanished as a large cloud sent the winter sun scurrying back to its hibernation. A visual gloom settled on the pair, as the mental one had moments before.

They sat in silence each in their own thoughts, yet not alone with them, sharing a common grief. The Old Man continued to rock gently. Nicky had seen many children do it, and quite a few adults in moments of grief or stress. It must give them comfort. Perhaps he should try it one day.

He broke the silence.

"I'll leave you in peace for a while, but this changes things. I suppose I already had a vested interest getting to the bottom of who was behind the attacks, knowing so many of you as I do, but now, after this, I feel it's personal."

The Old Man turned to him, his eyes glistening with moisture.

"You're too bloody nice to be a newspaper reporter, son. There can't be many like you. God bless you, lad. God bless you."

He rose abruptly and hobbled to the churchyard gates, leaving Nicky on the bench, shaking his head in disbelief over the news he'd just received.

CHAPTER ELEVEN

What the hell were the neighbours doing banging on the wall at this time of the morning? Grease rolled over and pulled the bedclothes over his head. Jeez, the bed stank. He couldn't remember the last time he changed the sheets. He couldn't be arsed. He couldn't be arsed about most things, especially at this time of day on a Saturday.

"Grease, open up."

He realised the hammering was coming from the front door, not the walls. He rolled out of bed, cursing. Without thinking, he reached for the pack of cigarettes on the bedside cabinet, which competed for space with the overflowing ashtray and empty beer cans.

The hammering continued.

"Alright, alright. Keep yer bloody knickers on. I'm coming."

He made his way to the front door in his boxers, coughing harshly as he inhaled a lungful of smoke. He could see a figure through the frosted glass. It was Jakey. He pulled back the chain and opened up.

ELEVEN

"What the fu..?"

"He's dead," Jakey shouted as he burst through the door.

"Why don't you shout a bit louder? I don't think they heard you down at Limehouse nick. Who's dead?"

Jakey started to pace around the living room, clutching his head, kicking discarded pizza boxes out of the way.

"What are we going to do?"

"To start with you're going to shut it, and then you're going to tell me what the fuck you're rattling on about."

Jakey stopped his pacing for a moment and took a deep breath.

"That crusty, last night at the canal. He's dead. I heard it on the news in the caff this morning."

"Shit."

"Yeah that just about covers it, Grease. We're going to get nicked for murder. Shit is right."

"Sit down and shut up. Yer doing my head in. I need to think."

Jakey tipped a pile of dirty clothes off the chair and sat with his face in his hands, rocking backwards and forwards.

"Okay, here's what we're going to do. We get rid of everything we had on Thursday night, right? I mean rid of it, every last stitch. Stick it in a bin bag and shove it in someone's bin. They can't pin it on us if they have no evidence."

"What if someone saw us?"

"No one saw us. You know there was no one around, and he never made a sound. Even if someone did see us they wouldn't be able to identify us. It was dark and we had our hoodies on. Once we get rid of them we'll get some different ones and there'll be no danger of being identified."

Jakey stopped rocking for a moment and lifted his head.

"I'm shit scared, Grease."

"Snap out of it, man. There's no way they can pin it on us. We'll let things die down for a while and then we'll get back to the business of getting rid of these homeless scum."

Jakey stared at him for a moment, shaking his head.

"You must be mad if you think we can carry on after that."

"It'll be fine, trust me."

Jakey continued his stare. "I want out, Grease. I'm not doing it anymore. It's one thing smacking people around a bit, persuading 'em to move on, find somewhere else. But murder? No way man. I'm not getting involved in that."

Grease sighed. "You already are, you arse. Just remember that. You want out? Fine. I'll find someone else, but you keep your trap shut, right? I go down, you go with me. Understand?"

Jakey jumped to his feet and dashed out of the door, slamming it behind him.

Stubbing his cigarette out on the top of an empty beer can, Grease let out another sigh and went back to the bedroom. No sense in being up this early. Christ, it's not even midday.

HARRY

CHAPTER TWELVE

Jeez it was cold. Not the frosty, burn your skin type of cold, but the sitting around doing nothing type. The sort that would seep into the bones and freeze the marrow. He didn't know how these people slept out here. Give him a warm cosy bed any night.

He wasn't sure why he'd come up with this plan, after all, what did he care if one or two of the crusties got a little thumped around. Then he recalled the one who had died. An ex-soldier by all accounts. More importantly, a white ex-soldier, and that made all the difference. One of his group would catch them at it and they would take the law into their own hands. The law? Pah! The law did absolutely nothing to stop it. The attacks had been going on for months and what had they done? Sweet FA, that's what. Sitting in warm offices drinking coffee, eating doughnuts, watching telly no doubt, while these innocent white folks, decent men and women, are getting their heads kicked in.

Well, all that would stop. BARE would show the people of Tower Hamlets it was a force to be reckoned

TWELVE

with. Any of you foreign scum step out of line and you'll get what's coming to you.

Leslie longed to stamp his feet to improve his circulation, but couldn't make a sound for fear of giving his position away to the scumbags, that's if they were around. No. Better to sit quietly and freeze, rather than scare them off. He wanted to catch them in the act.

A shadow moved on the path, a lone, long, dancing shadow. Somebody was coming; his shadow a precursor to the main event. Leslie hoped this was it. He could be a hero. Imagine how that would look in the paper. 'White Supremacist Leader catches killer.' Now wouldn't that be something?

Gotchya. A young Asian lad: he knew it would be one of them.

To Leslie's surprise, hands in pockets, the young lad continued past the figure lying asleep on the bench. A few paces further he hesitated, turning back towards him, hesitating once more before retracing his steps back to the man.

As he bent over the sleeper to take a better look, Leslie was on him in a flash, hitting him on the back of the head and knocking him to the ground.

"What you doing, asshole?"

The young Asian looked up. "I... I wasn't doing anything. I was just wanted to make sure he was okay."

Leslie shook his head. "You were going to smack him one weren't you? Why else would you be here?"

The young man sat up and held his hands, palms out, in a gesture of openness.

"I wasn't going to touch him, honest. I just wanted to make sure he was okay. I missed my bus and this is a shortcut home. I live in Mossford..."

He never got to finish the sentence before Leslie punched him, knocking him back to the floor. Never one to miss an opportunity to take advantage of someone in a less fortunate position than himself, he started to kick the young man where he lay. He didn't care where he kicked him, several of the blows landing on the boy's face. All the while he hurled abuse at him.

After working out his anger and frustration on the unfortunate youth, Leslie stopped. Panting heavily in the cold night air, he looked around. Not a soul to be seen. Good, not everybody understood the need to rid the earth of these scum. This one at least had been taught a lesson to remember, now maybe he would go back to whatever country he came from. Not for one moment did it cross his mind that England was his country and London his home. After all, how could it be? He wasn't even white.

ooOoo

The exchange of words woke the Old Man. Who on earth would be shouting at this time of night? What this time of night was he wasn't exactly sure, but he'd been on the streets long enough to know the city sounds and he guessed this would be what some people called the 'wee hours.' Normally he would ignore any altercation on the streets: usually they were something and nothing and blew over in a matter of minutes, but this sounded serious. The discussion appeared to be somewhat one-sided and although he was unable to hear all of the words, from what he could hear, and the tone, it suggested to him that someone had a lot of anger towards ethnic groups.

Sighing loudly in the manner of someone who would rather stay where they were, but had to be somewhere else, the Old Man pushed the newspaper 'quilt' to one side and set off towards the racket. He arrived in time to see a figure aiming a kick at a someone prone on the ground, take a look around him then run off in the direction of Mile End Road; his face briefly illuminated by the nearby

TWELVE

streetlamp. The Old Man crossed to the person lying on the ground. A young Asian, clearly unconscious, looked to be in a bad way. The swelling in both eyes kept them firmly closed; blood oozed from his nose and another trickle from a swollen lip; his breathing laboured.

Amazingly, someone still slept on the bench next to the victim. The Old Man took a quick glance at him. Ah, no wonder; Pete the Pole. There would be nothing out of him for the rest of the night. Somehow Pete always managed to get hold of enough vodka to pickle himself for a few hours. He could wait. The only medical treatment he needed would be paracetamol in the morning, and a liver transplant in the near future. This lad needed help now.

He checked him for any serious bleeding or broken bones; at least two ribs as far as he could tell. He rolled the unconscious figure into the recovery position as gently as he possibly could. Although it had been many years since he'd put it into practice, he remembered how to do that and he knew he couldn't leave the boy lying on his back on his own. It wouldn't take him long to choke on his own blood. At least now anything in his mouth would drain out.

He didn't like to leave the lad unattended, but he required professional help. The Old Man moved as quickly as he could to the call box outside the Britannia Fish Bar in Grove Road, a hundred metres or so from the park.

Ambulance summoned, he returned to the young lad who by now was moaning on the ground; he felt staying with him was the least he could do until the emergency services arrived. After what seemed to be hours but must have only been a matter of minutes, flashing blue lights at the park entrance announced the arrival of the first vehicle.

The Old Man retreated into the shadows and observed as

the paramedics tended to the unconscious figure. From the snatches of conversation he could hear, the lad was in a bad way. It wasn't right. No one should have to suffer that for the colour of their skin, or for any other reason for that matter. The world was a screwed up place.

HARRY

CHAPTER THIRTEEN

Twenty hours straight she'd been working on this code, but it would be worthwhile. Even as a child she wanted to know everything, especially when it didn't concern her. Now in her mid-twenties, she'd amassed a formidable battery of technology, not to mention the skill sets to access places she shouldn't and see things she ought not to.

0rchid hacked, not in the physical world with axes or large knives, but in that mysterious space called the 'net' and with computers. 0rchid engaged in white-hat hacking. She snooped around looking for juicy information, then did nothing; no damage to the system, no malicious code or viruses, no posting the contents on bulletin boards; just plain old fashioned snooping. While she saw nothing wrong with this, there were many, including the law, who did not agree, so she made certain she covered her tracks with never less than five VPNs and all manner of modern wizardry connecting to her personal botnet in Russia, keeping her identity secret. Of course, 0rchid wasn't her real name, but the handle she used in the hacking

THIRTEEN

community. Not the place to advertise either your real name, or anything else that would lead the authorities to your door.

The code in front of her came from a fellow hacker by the name of Jack Sparrow. She only ever met him online and had no idea what he looked like. Her assumption was of a spotty teenager with thick glasses and floppy hair, at least he acted that way; a bit childish at times. He might be clever with coding, clever might be an understatement, but his handle might not be so if he followed the Pirates of the Caribbean films. Never use a handle that relates to you in any way. She chose 0rchid at random, and in the way of many hackers, substituted a number for one of the letters. She didn't even like flowers.

Sparrow's code, as good as it was, wouldn't quite be up to what she intended, and he knew it, which is why he passed it on to 0rchid. He acknowledged her superior skills. Sparrow had been unable to find a way past one of the security levels without giving the game away. 0rchid believed she might have the answer so he gave up the code to her in the hopes she could achieve the unachievable.

Hacking into the government run GCHQ was reputed to be well-nigh impossible, and especially risky given that it was their job to snoop on others. The words risk and impossible only made her all the more determined to be the first to do so. She needed to clear many layers of protection and alarms if she were to hit the top prize. She didn't intend doing anything once inside, the mere fact she hacked into the UK's communication centre would put her at the top of her game. Of course, she would never be able to tell anyone she had cracked the prize nut, except Jack Sparrow himself maybe. Many a hacker had been caught not from their efforts to gain access, but from bragging about it once they achieved their goal. Keep low, stay quiet: that had to be the only way to operate.

Aware of the immense risk, she still felt the tingle of

anticipation when gaining access to something of this magnitude. With this code she would break in stealthily, have a nose around and come out again without them ever knowing of her intrusion. She must get this right. Any stray code may trigger their defences and they would be on to her. She flicked her long blond hair out of her face, tucking it behind her ears, the monitor reflecting in her blue eyes as she stared intently into the screen. Perhaps she should try to sleep and start afresh tomorrow. She wouldn't; with the prize in her reach now, she had to push on. If all went well, next weekend would be the one.

CHAPTER FOURTEEN

"So he became a high-flying reporter while I rotted away in jail because of him, eh?"

His companion nodded while taking a swig of his beer, swallowed, then burped loudly.

"Sorry. Yeah, that's about the size of it."

A roar came from the group playing darts in the corner, someone just scored a hundred and eighty.

Munro glared in their direction then returned to his conversation.

"He'll be sorry when I get my hands on him. Aye, and whoever nicked the stuff from ma office." He clenched his jaw. "That was my retirement plan. Now look at me, an old lag with nothing. Not even a bloody family. Gone, all of it. Gone."

Munro's eyes were glassy, staring into the distance. A vein in his temple pulsed in time with his heartbeat. For the past twenty-five years he thought about nothing but the man whose testimony put him inside. When he got word his offices and entire stock had been cleaned out,

FOURTEEN

that was the last straw. Someone would pay, and pay dearly. No one crossed Donald Munro and got away scot-free.

Prison made time hang heavily. Time that could turn brooding into bitterness, and bitterness into bile, poisoning the soul. There were many who considered Munro did not possess a soul, nevertheless, prison poisoned him, filling him with anger and hatred. In the past, anyone who crossed him met an untimely end, well, that had been business hadn't it? - nothing personal. This was personal; that man Rolands would know what it was like to hurt.

At least he knew one of the people on whom he should focus his hatred, and he harboured strong suspicions about another.

"And Morvern, where is he now?"

"No one's seen neither hide nor hair of him since the day you were arrested. Not heard a peep. As if he fell off the face of the earth."

Munro gaze shifted to his pint, his eyes seemingly focused in the distance, but he didn't see his drink; he saw darkness, a darkness welling up from deep within his psyche, and in the darkness he could see revenge, revenge being the sole light, and he fluttered to the light, as a moth to a flame.

"He's out there somewhere, with my money. I can feel it. It couldn't be anyone else; the rest were rounded up - he was the only one who wasn't. Then there was the business with the money for the diamond deal. He thought that cock and bull story of a switch somewhere had me fooled, but I know it was him. I know it."

Once again, the pair lapsed into silence, staring into their glasses, as is often the way for two people who have known each other for a long time. A conversation did not always involve words.

HARRY

At one time the pair pretty much ran London's East End underworld between them, and although adversaries, they never warred with each other, preferring instead to avoid confrontation; keeping things professional and courteous at all times. This led to the building of a relationship based on mutual respect, as much as criminals can respect each other.

Munro avoided the clutches of the law for many years, until that fateful 'investment' in some conflict diamonds from Angola. Munro ran a legitimate business in gemstones, turning a good profit in its own right, as well as using it as a front for his more clandestine operations. He jumped at the chance to buy Angolan diamonds at a knock-down price. Greed once again overcoming common sense. Unfortunately, the deal went wrong resulting in him losing several million pounds, in cash and bearer-bonds.

On top of his conviction for Conspiracy to Murder, having ordered the 'disposal' of a snooping reporter, Nicky Rolands, Munro was handed another for handling counterfeit notes, but that was another story.

The result of all this being a minimum tariff of twenty-five years, which he served in prisons scattered around the UK, finally returning to London and the Belmarsh Prison, before release on licence and an eventual return to the East End, a broken man. Both mentally and physically he became a shadow of his former self. In his own environment Munro had been a keep fit fanatic and mentally agile, but prison left its mark.

Many of Munro's enemies, those not languishing at the bottom of the Thames, were in the prison system. He spent a lot of his time evading their clutches. For some, incarceration can set them straight, for others it is considered a hazard of the job, and for a few, the introspection it can foster becomes a corrosive poison in their minds.

FOURTEEN

Munro believed he was far too clever to be caught, and for many years he had been. Until that Nicky Rolands came along and ruined his life. A still-wet-behind-the-ears youngster, nothing more, and yet he took away everything he had. Never mind the fact he hadn't personally taken anything, he had been the root cause: that was enough. Day in, day out, Munro would see Rolands' name in the paper, either as a reporter, or later as an editor. The steady drip-drip-drip of acid that was Nicky Rolands, fed on Munro, torturing his soul, slowly devouring him until all that remained was the image of Rolands' neck in his hands as he slowly squeezed the life out of him.

CHAPTER FIFTEEN

As Nicky left the churchyard he reflected on the conversation with the Old Man. The news of the murder put a different light on things. This was no longer a story about the cruelty of man, this was about the inhumanity of man. What drove people to attack others? What existed in the human psyche that made them so aggressive to their fellow man? He didn't understand it.

Nicky made a beeline for the Docklands Light Railway station a couple of hundred metres away. At this time of day Bow Road was busy, but the traffic hardly registered with him, nor the pedestrians around him; encapsulated in his own little world. Normally the ambling type, he found himself almost running. Perhaps he was running; running away from what he just learned.

A few years earlier, Nicky spent some time with the homeless, writing a political article about housing policy in the UK. In that time, he became a nodding acquaintance of many of the homeless people, and with a few, like the Old Man, he developed a much closer relationship, which he maintained. Brian had been one of those too. Not as

FIFTEEN

close as the Old Man, but enough to feel the pain of the loss.

The Old Man - how strange in all this time he never found out his real name? When Nicky first asked, the Old Man told him he didn't need to know, and he soon found out everyone else referred to him as the Old Man anyway.

He must go back to the office. This was a new story, a much bigger story than the one he'd been sent to investigate. A life had been lost, the life of someone Nicky considered to be more than merely an acquaintance. He would put himself on the story and follow it through to the bitter end.

If that ass of an editor doesn't like it, he can 'stick his job where the sun don't shine.' Nicky's reputation would land him a job almost anywhere, and freelancing was always an option. The more he thought about it, the more he realised this job was coming to its natural conclusion and the idea of freelance work looked downright attractive. Set your own hours and pursue your own interests. He had enough money set aside to not have to worry when the next pay cheque would arrive. This could well be his last article for this paper as an employee. Back to the task in hand, once he sorted out the editor he would hit the streets. His time spent with the homeless would give him an edge; people would open up to him far more than the police.

As he entered the station, it struck him on this occasion he should bow to technology. Why waste time going back, isn't that why they invented the mobile? Nicky still lived in the past when it came to gadgets. He had his PC for setting up his copy, but when taking notes in the outside world, he much preferred a notebook made from chopped up trees, and writing with a pencil, because pens won't write on wet paper. That is something you learn at 1 a.m., trying to write down details of a major breaking story in the pouring rain. You only make the mistake once. You don't ever want to be on the receiving end of a bollocking like that again when your editor discovers what you've done, and because another paper publishes an exclusive as a result of your inability to read your own notes. Nicky still used shorthand whenever he needed to, yet another skill he learned early in his career.

'Let's see the rivals hack into that from their offices,' he told others when they asked why he didn't embrace the 'labour saving' technology available to him. Too many journalists these days tried to obtain news the easy way. Hacking phones, computers and emails was downright lazy in his book, not to mention being slightly on the wrong side of the law. Besides, the battery never goes flat on a paper notebook.

Nicky thought back to his early days as a cub reporter, he wasn't even sure if they used the term these days. The youngsters coming through to the papers now, already knew all there was to know, after all they held degrees in Media Studies or Journalism, so why wouldn't they? He smiled to himself. The optimism of youth. They soon learned theory and practice can often be widely differing things. Some realised they still had much to learn, they were the ones destined to go on to bigger and better things. The ones with an uncle who owned a publication or two bypassed the learning process of course.

He took his mobile out of his pocket and tried to remember how to unlock the screen. Many prods, swipes and stabs later he reached the editor's voicemail. Handy. No discussion. Leave a message and job done. Call made, he switched off his phone so he didn't have to waste time arguing with his boss later.

He set about formulating a plan to find out who had committed this vile act. Somebody, somewhere must have seen something. One snippet that would be all he needed to get started. As he stood on the bridge looking down on the Docklands Light Railway, it struck him he knew just

FIFTEEN

the place to get the ball rolling. A train pulled into the station, and as there is no time like the present, Nicky rushed down the ramp to the platform, swiping his travel pass and boarding seconds before the doors closed. Minutes later he stepped off the train at Canary Wharf. He would speak with someone from his past; someone with whom he hadn't spoken for twenty-five years.

CHAPTER SIXTEEN

The Canary Wharf business district in London covers a substantial part of the former West India Docks in the East End. Mention Canary Wharf to the average person and they will think of one particular building, One Canada Square. For ten years the distinctive shape on the London skyline remained the tallest building in the UK, until The Shard knocked it from the top spot. At one time Nicky had been a regular visitor to the iconic building; the Daily Telegraph occupied six floors for a number of years. It was on one of those visits he spotted someone he thought he recognised. His appearance had changed from how Nicky remembered him, but nevertheless remained convinced it was the same person. By doing a bit of detective work he established the name this person was now going by. He surmised if he went to the trouble of changing his appearance and name, then Nicky would not be a welcome visitor, so he let things be and made no further enquiries. Eventually, the Telegraph relocated elsewhere and he had no further reason to visit the building.

SIXTEEN

Today he was going to change all of that and put his suspicions to the test. By a mixture of flashing his press pass, charm and good old fashioned bluffing, he managed to get past security and make his way to the offices of one of the very first tenants of the building, a gemstone dealer, the only one in the tower. The merchant was in for a bit of a surprise, possibly even a shock, but Nicky hoped he would help track down those responsible for the recent attacks on the homeless, and therefore Brian's murderer.

Any casual observer might wonder why a man of such repute as this well-established merchant would need such knowledge, but he hadn't always been so brightly polished. If Nicky was right, the man had a somewhat murky past, one which entangled Nicky some twenty-five years earlier. Despite this less than salubrious history, he would be in no danger; the man was no threat to him; if he was right, they grew up together and had previously enjoyed a reasonably good relationship. Even the events of nineteen-ninety had not been of the man's making.

Leonard Stone - Gemstones announced a modest sign on the opaque glass door of the office suite. Nicky opened it to reveal a middle-aged lady sitting at a reception desk, who smiled politely and asked Nicky how she could help.

"I'd like to see Mr Stone please."

"Do you have an appointment, Mr...err?"

Nicky shook his head as he fished inside his jacket pocket.

"Then I'm afraid you will..."

Nicky handed over his business card. "Please give that to Mr Stone. I can assure you he will want to see me. I'll wait over here shall I?"

The receptionist gave him a frosty look as only a receptionist can as she picked up the telephone on her desk, jabbed a single button and after a brief pause announced Nicky's presence to the person on the other end. Her eyebrows took a journey up her forehead as she acknowledged the response with a curt, "Yes, sir."

She rose from her desk, took the ten or so paces to the large mahogany door set behind and to one side of her desk, knocked, waited a moment, then entered the inner sanctum.

Moments later she returned and motioned Nicky to join her.

"You are very fortunate. Mr Stone is free at the moment and will see you right away."

Nicky refrained from saying, 'Told you so', but his sweet smile said it anyway.

The outer office had been simply decorated; simple but not cheap; done by someone who understood style and elegance. The elegant, but now not quite so simple, theme continued in the office he now entered. A highly polished mahogany conference table, big enough to seat ten, occupied the space to the right of the door. White leather covered chairs accompanied the table, complimented by a large four seater white leather settee which faced the enormous mahogany desk positioned close to the floor-to-ceiling windows. Two matching armchairs were arranged at ninety degrees to one side of the sofa. Beyond the desk Nicky could see an outstanding view of London City Airport, far better than from any of the former offices of the Daily Telegraph, as it should, being some twenty floors higher. It gave Nicky a touch of vertigo. Behind the desk, looking out of the window and with his back to Nicky, stood a tall figure. He watched a Flybe Dash 8 climbing away from the airport, until it went out of sight to the left of the building, and a few hundred feet higher.

"I could watch those all day, if I didn't have work to do." He turned towards Nicky.

"What can I do for you, Mr.." he glanced at the business card in his hand, "...Rolands?"

SIXTEEN

Nicky smiled. "Lenny, cut the crap. I know it's you and I've known for years. I saw you in the lobby once, it was a good few years ago, mind you. I knew it was you even then, though you looked different to the Lenny I remembered. A bit of snooping around and I was pretty certain it was you, though I admit you covered your tracks well. Plastic surgery?"

Twenty seconds of silence is a long time. Finally, Leonard Stone gestured toward the sofa. "Take a seat, Nicky boy."

If there were any lingering doubts in Nicky's mind about the true identity of this man, that one phrase swept them away. No one else ever referred to him as 'Nicky boy.'

"What are you after?"

That threw Nicky. It wasn't the first time he'd gone off on a whim without any real plan, but this time he didn't have the vaguest idea where to start. His expertise lay in catching politicians and prominent people doing things they shouldn't. He already knew who his targets were, where to start looking and what to look for. His experience of criminal investigation was limited, and probably highly coloured by the fictitious offerings on the TV. With no reference point from which to start he was lost. So he did the only thing he could and started the story from the beginning, when he first met the rough sleepers.

Lenny listened without interruption for almost twenty minutes until Nicky finished his story.

"What on earth have you got yourself into this time, Nicky?"

Nicky shrugged his shoulders and Lenny continued.

"I'm still not sure what you want from me."

"Help. Help me to find this person, or these people, before someone else dies. You must still know people in the borough."

Lenny stared out the window as another aircraft climbed steeply away.

"What about the police?"

"They're working on it but it's early days. In the meantime, someone else may die. You can talk to people they can't. They'll tell you things they won't tell the police."

Lenny continued watching the aircraft until it was out of sight.

"I'm not that person any more, Nicky boy. I left all that behind when I came here. I don't move in those circles now, it was a means to an end, and the end was achieved when Munro got his come-uppance. Speaking of which, I hear he's looking for you. The years inside turned him into a twisted wretch of a man; he wants revenge. He's looking for me too, so I hear, but I'm more difficult to find." He stopped for a moment. "Well, at least I thought so until you waltzed through that door."

Nicky smiled weakly. "I'm a reporter, it's my job to find out things people don't want found." He looked at his hands for a few moments before continuing, "You say you don't move in those circles, yet you tell me Munro is on the lookout for me. You must still have contacts, Lenny, otherwise how would you know?"

Lenny sighed. "As sharp as ever I see, Nicky boy. You're right, I have one or two people I trust who are still connected to that life. Like you, they recognised me, but I would trust them with my life, in fact I suppose that is exactly what I'm doing now Munro is out." He rubbed his forehead with two fingers. "I'll see what I can do, but I can't make any promises and I won't do anything to compromise my position any more than it already is. Lenny Morvern disappeared the day Munro was arrested. I intend to keep it that way as much as I possibly can."

SIXTEEN

He stood, and Nicky took his cue the meeting was over. Lenny escorted Nicky to the door.

Nicky put out his hand and they shook. "That's all I can ask for, Lenny. That's all I can ask for."

Lenny put his hand on Nicky's shoulder "Watch your back, Nicky boy. He's out there and he wants your hide."

Nicky nodded in acknowledgement as he made his way to the outer office. As he walked past the receptionist he gave her a wink, which she studiously ignored with a polite, "Good day to you, sir."

CHAPTER SEVENTEEN

Lenny went back to his desk, sat rather clumsily in his office chair, kicked off his shoes and put his feet up. He stared at the door for several seconds while his mind churned things over. At first his decision had been to do nothing. Why should he? He had his own business and was well off. Loving wife, 2.2 children, well, three to be exact, and it wasn't the proverbial Volvo in his drive, but an Aston Martin Vantage. Okay, so he did get a head start by liberating Munro's assists, but after that he had been legal and fair in his dealings. He had turned Munro's small fortune into a much larger one. Something Munro would have been able to do if he hadn't been so obsessed with trying to con people and shady deals.

So why should he help find the killer of this homeless person? Lenny thought about it, and that was his mistake, because the more he thought about it, the more he got drawn in. All these years as a journalist, a pretty powerful one at that, Nicky boy kept shtum. He could have tipped of any number of people as to his real identity, but he didn't. Nor did he try to cash in on it in some way, at least not until now; and he was hardly cashing in. No threats of revealing his true identity, just a heartfelt plea for help.

That meant a lot to Lenny. As tough as he could be, Lenny still had a heart. He and Nicky went back a long way, as far as junior school, only going their separate ways when Lenny left school to go into his father's business. Yes, Nicky not only deserved his support, he deserved his protection. Unlike Munro, Lenny didn't keep a small army of minders; he didn't need to. He wasn't in the habit of stepping on the toes of people who would chop off your hands for doing so. That would mean doing the protection himself and what better time than right now.

Slipping his shoes back on he raced out of his office yelling to his secretary to cancel all meetings for the foreseeable future. There was no time to lose in making sure Nicky boy got to see another day.

HARRY

CHAPTER EIGHTEEN

He lay on his bed, eyes fixed firmly on the ceiling, hands clasped over his head, resting lightly on the pillow; his breathing shallow and fast. The palms of his hands glistened with sweat and trickles ran from his forehead; rivulets seeking the comfort of the pillow. This was a place he had not been for some time. The primal feelings welled up, threatening to take over his higher reasoning. No, not just threatening, overwhelming, like an emotional Armageddon. Twenty-five years ago these feeling surfaced and he gave in to them. Since then he had learned to suppress them, hide them away, shield society from his dark side, but now was the time to allow those thoughts and desires to surface. The last time, it was for survival; kill or be killed. This time his physical survival would not be in question; he had nothing to fear in this city or on these streets.

Brian too had served in the military, did his duty, and like Harry, well, like many of them, he found himself without a job. 'Cutbacks,' they said, 'you do understand, nothing we can do.' And that's that. Abandoned by the

EIGHTEEN

service to which you dedicated the best years of your life, and abandoned by successive governments to fend for yourself. Give yourself to Queen and Country, then be left to rot on the streets when your usefulness ended. Who would have thought that servicemen would be part of a throwaway society? The latest insult to these brave men and women, a bunch of lawyers, pursuing former servicemen for alleged war crimes: a sniper for not shouting a warning before firing; a soldier for shooting someone shooting at him. Good god, what next? - A government health warning to be printed on shell casings? He could see it now. *'Warning - this round may seriously harm your health, cause injury or even death. Stand in the way with care.'* The world had gone mad; the lunatics in charge of the asylum.

Harry had been fortunate, or perhaps wiser than some. He kept his flat in London while he served, and a good thing too, otherwise he also would be living permanently on the streets; not necessarily a bad thing. After all, he still did from time to time, he liked the camaraderie; the nearest thing to being back in his squadron. Camaraderie was the thing servicemen missed the most. Civilians just didn't understand it, they were too wrapped up in their own lives to care about others, to have a sense of community, to know what it means to rely on the man next to you to keep you alive. Sure, you have a responsibility to keep yourself alive, but never at the expense of a comrade. There was no 'I' in team, as the instructors kept drilling into them. That suited Harry's philosophy perfectly, he was a pack animal after all.

Brian? - well he had no choice; he never owned any property and the streets became his only life after his service. He'd been no trouble to anyone. They never crossed paths while serving, but saw action in some of the same places, and like Harry, Brian put himself in harm's way on more than one occasion. Then the other night, someone took his life from him; beat it out of him while he slept. Is that any way to go? - and for what? So some low life could get their kicks picking on the homeless. Only this time they went too far. Someone would pay for that. Harry didn't care if they were the culprits or not. As long as they lived on the wrong side of the law, and Harry's definition could be quite loose, they would be on the receiving end of his justice. Brian's death had been pointless, even if his life had not been. That annoyed Harry the most, that Brian survived the battlefield only to die at the hands of some cowardly scum. Scum who probably never did a decent thing in their lives; high on drugs or drink, or maybe both, then seeking out someone defenceless to 'have a bit of fun.'

Harry sighed, this wound him up. The more he thought, the more the anger took hold. Brian belonged to his pack; no one attacked Harry's pack and got away with it. He'd not been spending as much time on the streets recently, well it was time to change that. To some, sleeping rough meant a camper van, fully equipped with microwave and shower, but Harry knew the true meaning. To him it was freedom, free from the trappings of a modern world, free to be himself. He wasn't a true rough sleeper, he knew that. He still had his apartment to go back to, but at least when he felt hemmed in by those four walls he had the option to make the city his living room.

He picked up a book and found his page. To Harry, reading provided a means to escape this world and immerse himself in another. A world where anything and everything was possible and he could be safe. No one could reach him there. His interest in sci-fi from such authors as Asimov, Arthur C Clarke and Alan Dean Foster, would come as a surprise to many, given his devotion to the Bible. Very few knew this side of him, not even the few whom he called friends. And as a fan of Star Wars he fully understood what they meant by 'the dark

EIGHTEEN

side' of the force. It held with his own beliefs of good and evil. Now it was time for him to once again turn to his own dark side and clear the streets of these creatures. Too many people lived off the efforts of others. Leeches, one and all. They would pay and he would rejoice, the perfect balance.

His breathing slowed, becoming deeper and relaxed; the yoga training taking over; the military training would be used later. Tonight he would start his search for those for whom the payback was due.

Revenge of the Sith would have nothing on the retribution he would inflict on those unfortunate enough to come to his attention.

CHAPTER NINETEEN

The Tower Hamlets district of London could not be considered the most sensible place in the world to hand out leaflets discussing white supremacy, but Leslie believed if you were white, you had the right. White British now only made up thirty-one per cent of the population in this area, and Leslie intended to bring it to the attention of anyone who would listen. His aim was not only to stop the trend but to reverse it until the whites once again became the majority group, or indeed, the only group. He felt outraged that successive governments allowed Bangladeshis, of all people, to become the dominant group in an area he considered to be part of the backbone of London, the East End. Londoners, who remained steadfast during the blitz had now succumbed to an invasion by stealth. Not once did it cross his mind he would be part of the remaining sixty-nine per cent of that statistic as even though he was white, he wasn't British.

Always aware of the possibility of trouble, Leslie ensured at least two of his more capable followers stayed with him whenever he ventured out on one of his crusades. By capable he meant troublemakers, handy in a scrap and not fearful of being arrested; something not unknown to them.

The Tesco Express on Mile End Road was one of his favourite places, mainly because he could point to the road behind and tell them it was named British Street for a reason. He was happy to press his leaflets on both whites and the 'other lot,' as he liked to call them. They needed to know that their days were numbered. On more than one occasion this led to some heated exchanges of opinion that would be brought to an abrupt end when one of the heavies stepped in to persuade the other party it was time to leave. Usually this would be achieved by sticking a large pudgy face inches from the other person and yelling, "Fuck off...now." So far, everyone had taken the hint and moved several feet away at least before hurling their own abuse as they beat a hasty retreat.

Today the leaflets extolled the superiority of whites in all respects, and how every non-white should be repatriated, at their own expense of course, to whatever nation they originated, thus freeing up jobs and housing for those who deserved it. As was usual, there was printed at the bottom of the leaflet a contact email address, for anyone who wished to attend one of the weekly meetings to discuss what should be done to rid this green and pleasant land of the blight of non-whites.

A heated conversation peaked rapidly and edged towards the brink of a pudgy-faced intervention. No one noticed the tall, stringy looking man pick up the leaflet that moments ago had been thrown to the floor after it had been thrust into the hands of an elderly middle-eastern gentleman.

The tall man scanned the leaflet and made a mental note of the email address before discarding it in the waste bin adjacent to the Coburn Road bus-stop. This meeting might be right up his street. He would have to consult his social diary of course, but he believed Thursday night may well be a practical proposition. He could hardly wait.

CHAPTER TWENTY

Harry wasn't in the least bit surprised when he saw the pub. A typical drinking house in a London backstreet. This wasn't one of your modern chain run, family establishments, restaurants with a bar; this was more the sort of place that not too long ago would have had sawdust on the floor, swept out nightly, along with the odd drunk or two. The function room on the first floor came as no surprise either; wooden floorboards, cheap wooden chairs and tables and a small stage at one end. No doubt on a Saturday night the clientele would be under-dressed and over made-up teenage girls, coyly avoiding the testosterone and alcohol fuelled young lads with a pocketful of condoms, in case they got lucky; all bouncing around the floor to the ungodly sound that passed itself off as music these days.

The room hardly thronged with people when Harry walked in. In fact, there were so few in attendance his presence drew attention immediately. A scruffy looking young man with unkempt blond hair broke away from his conversation with what could only be described as a large genetic throwback, and swaggered across the room to introduce himself.

"Welcome, I'm Andrew Leslie, leader of BARE. I take it that's why you're here, Mr...err?"

"Harry. Yes, yes it is."

"Ah you're the guy who emailed this week, right? Harry...you have a last name?"

The guy that emailed? Clearly the general public were not in a rush to become members.

"I do, Mr Leslie, but I'm keeping that to myself."

Leslie nodded. "I fully understand. It doesn't pay to give too much away these days. You never know who is watching."

Harry smiled as he thought, you're not wrong there, sonny Jim.

Leslie reached out a hand and welcomed Harry to his first meeting of BARE where they would introduce him to their ideas for giving Britain back to the white Anglo-Saxons.

"Correct me if I'm wrong, Mr Leslie, but I'm detecting an antipodean accent there. I suspect you aren't Anglo-Saxon yourself."

Despite having two hefty 'bouncers' handy, Harry could see Leslie weighing up the pros and cons of getting into any sort of altercation with him. Harry found this stimulating, in a perverse way. The man was so full of confidence; most of it arising from the knowledge he had muscle to protect him if things went awry. This time discretion won and Leslie responded without malice.

"I might be from Australia but my ancestors are from here, so I have the country at heart."

Harry wondered if Leslie ever had a job working with the public as his smile was that of someone who is used to doing it for a living, and if Leslie's ancestors travelled to Australia willingly, or in the nineteenth century; an all-expenses paid trip in shackles, courtesy of the British Government.

"I'll take your word for that, Mr Leslie, and I'll see what you have to say, before I make up my mind."

Leslie smiled again.

"So you are thinking of joining us."

Harry looked him straight in the eye.

"Like I said, that remains to be seen."

Leslie studied him for several seconds before deciding not to press the point and turning abruptly away to take his place on the small stage.

Harry expected a lacklustre performance and Leslie did not disappoint him. If this was the standard of rhetoric from a self-proclaimed leader of a white supremacist group, then the non-whites had nothing to fear. Most of what he said, Harry had heard before from many of the extremist groups claiming to represent the interests of the country, or the people, or the future of their children, or any number of other reasons, when their only real interest was perpetuating their own distorted views of the world. Leslie's rehash provided nothing new, and to Harry's ears the whole speech sounded contrived and unconvincing. On the other hand, some of the monobrows in the audience were lapping it up, nodding their heads and applauding at each outrageous statement. You can lead a horse to knowledge, but you can't make it think.

As Leslie spoke his drivel, Harry discreetly scanned the room. He would not have been surprised to find one or even several of this group of followers had been involved in the attacks on the homeless. They seemed to be the type who would enjoy inflicting injury on those unable to defend themselves. As Obi Wan Kenobi once said to Luke Skywalker in Star Wars, 'you will never find

TWENTY

a more wretched hive of scum and villainy.' Although Harry knew you could find far worse in any number of places in the borough, the line from the movie seemed appropriate in the circumstances. These scum hated people without any other reason than because someone told them to. Harry found this difficult to understand.

The meeting drew to a close and several of the attendees milled around to speak to Leslie, occasionally glancing in Harry's direction, suspicious of the newcomer. After speaking to several, Leslie made a beeline for Harry.

"So, what do you think?"

What Harry thought would be the last thing Leslie would want to hear, so he kept things vague.

"You gave me something to think about."

Desperate to gain a new supporter for his group, Leslie missed the undertones in Harry's words.

"So, we'll see you again?"

"Oh, you'll see me again, Mr Leslie. You can count on it."

This time Harry thought he detected the slightest flicker of doubt in Leslie's eyes. Perhaps he caught the undertone after all.

CHAPTER TWENTY-ONE

The lack of progress began to frustrate Helene. Other than the shoe prints, physical evidence from the murder scene matched nothing on the database, so that narrowed it down to wearers of size 10 Nike shoes. You might obtain all the evidence in the world, but unless you already have a suspect in custody, or something to match on a database, the investigation could not move forward.

Despite several violent attacks prior to the murder, they were still unable to find a single person who saw the attackers other than the victims themselves, and their statements proved useless: one, two or possibly more attackers, short, tall, black, white, Asian, stocky, thin, the list went on. The descriptions given varied so widely they had nothing concrete to go on. Only the evidence collected from the scene of the murder could be relied on, and that was getting them nowhere. The wood particles from the wall proved to be ash, one of the most widely used woods for manufacture of baseball bats; the polyurethane varnish common to more than one manufacturer.

TWENTY-ONE

"What are we missing, Davy? There must be something here. We're just not seeing it."

"I'm not so sure they meant to kill him Ma'am. After all, the way he died was accidental, the asphyxiation thingy."

"Positional."

"Yeah, that's the one. None of the blows would have been fatal from what I can gather from the PM report, so....," Davy stopped to gather his thoughts, "...if it was me, and I'd killed somebody by accident, I'd want to get rid of the evidence, clothing, weapon, etcetera."

"You wouldn't give yourself up then?"

Davy turned quickly to his boss and noted the twinkle in her eye.

"Just pulling your plonker, Davy."

An image flashed into Helene's mind and she dismissed it as quickly as it came. Not now, girl, and not ever here.

He continued. "As I was saying, Ma'am, I'd bin the evidence. Maybe we should tackle things from that angle."

Helene looked thoughtful. "We searched the immediate area and the canal, but as for other places, where do we start? And of course they may not have dumped it."

She studied at the evidence board, tapping her fingers on her chin, then cocked her head to one side.

"In the absence of anything else concrete to go on, let's start looking at some of the right wing groups. See if any of our contacts have heard anyone making a noise about people living on the streets. Has anyone had a run-in with one of the homeless; been bragging about their exploits? I think you might be right about it being accidental, but I still want to nail their balls to the wall. I'll clear things with DI Renton and let him know what I've asked you to do."

CHAPTER TWENTY-TWO

From an early age, Emma wanted a career in a bank. She thought there was something secure and proper about financial institutions and had she been born forty years earlier, that might have been the case. All through school, Emma's goal was to pursue her vision of her ideal career and chose her subjects at school to suit. By the time she graduated from the London School of Economics she realised what a ghastly mistake she'd made. Nevertheless, when she received an offer from one of the major banks in the City, she was thrilled. The position of Risk Analyst sounded to be an ideal opportunity for an adrenalin junkie, but she already knew by now, for her the work would be tedious, although other avenues could open up for her from the position.

Emma loved flirting with danger, and did so whenever she could, which on her salary was nowhere near as often as she would like. Living in London on a relatively low wage left her little cash to spare for regular pursuit of anything remotely risky, unless you counted a late night tube to Tower Hamlets as a dangerous pursuit.

TWENTY-TWO

An evening with mates in a wine bar close to work, saw her coming home a little later than expected. At the last moment she recognised the train was at her stop, Mile End. A moment sooner and she would have made it, but with the doors already closed the train rattled its way out of the station. Nothing for it but to get off at the next stop and walk back. The station at Bow Road wasn't much more of a walk anyway.

As she entered the Tower Hamlet's Cemetery Park, she had the feeling of being watched. She shrugged it off and carried on deeper into the park. A noise came from her left and with sudden clarity Emma remembered hearing about the serial rapist in the area; she fought off the urge to run. She didn't mind adrenalin, but not when associated with true fear.

She stopped and swung around. She couldn't see anyone on the path, but that didn't mean there wasn't somebody hiding in the bushes, or behind a headstone. Being in a cemetery after dark wouldn't normally worry her, not that she frequented them on a regular basis, and the thought of being surrounded by the dead didn't worry her at all. But on this occasion, she felt spooked. An overwhelming feeling of someone spying on her would not go away.

She quickened her pace as she moved into the centre of the park. Damn it, why did she have to miss her stop?

CHAPTER TWENTY-THREE

In common with most places of its kind, Tower Hamlets' Cemetery could not be described as fun place to be during the day, but at night it gained an extra creepiness. The majority of rough sleepers stayed away, the rustling of the trees in the darkness gave them the shivers, but on occasion a lone brave soul would chance their arm for a good night's kip. Not being the sort to scare easily, Harry belonged to that select group, as and when the mood suited him.

That wasn't to say the park would be empty after dark. Some used it as a shortcut, while others lingered a while longer. Harry often stumbled upon lovers, teenagers really, using the place for some illicit fumblings, even going all the way on occasion, on top of a convenient tomb, or in the grass. In other parts of the cemetery small groups of the living dead milled around. Not zombies of course, he didn't believe such things existed, but the druggies. Dark sunken eyes, pale parchment like skin, yellow teeth, scarred arms, one might well believe many of them had recently risen from a grave. Sadly, for many,

TWENTY-THREE

a journey in the other direction would be more likely to feature more prominently in their immediate future.

A muffled scream, one which was cut short, drew his attention. Screams were not an uncommon occurrence here, but this was different; not a scream of pleasure this time, but one of fear.

He moved rapidly toward the source of the sound. In the autumn these paths would be covered in leaves and fallen twigs, but at this time of year nothing lay to catch underfoot, except maybe the odd discarded aluminium drink can. A different story in the grass; condoms and syringes not an uncommon find. Nobody these days showed any respect for the dead; only to be expected, most of them didn't have any respect for the living either.

A low voice came from behind the bushes to one side of the path. Whispered threats and muffled sobs entwined in the darkness. Harry knew how to do this; the silent approach. He was good at this. The forces trained him well; it became second nature to him. Moving without a sound, he cautiously peered around the edge of the bush; his eyes now fully accustomed to the dark.

What he saw did not surprise him, but it did fill him with disgust. This was no lovers' tryst, or a quickie, not unless they were into some seriously dangerous role play, and the look in the girl's eyes; one of fear, not longing. A rape was in progress. He read the papers, and chances were that this was the man who featured on the front pages over the past few months; at least, the search for him had. Why did people not heed the warnings, especially the lone young females?

He felt in his pocket and searched the comforting touch of something familiar. His fingers caressed the wooden handles then dallied on the cold steel wire, almost stroking it. An inexplicable sense of calm washed over him; a calmness borne from familiarity. The wire was his friend, it never let him down. The wire belonged in his pack. Not since Kuwait had his friend been used in anger. Though on many occasions he had been tempted, he fought the urge, but now the urge would have its way; unleashed in all its glory. The pent up anger created by the death of Brian would be released. His friend would taste blood again, as would its close ally, the knife. The three of them made a formidable team.

The man pinning the girl to the ground was disadvantaged on three counts. His first - he had only one thing on his mind, his whole being focused on terrifying this girl and satisfying his own desires. His second - his hands were full; one held a knife to the girl's throat, with the other he attempted to undo his trousers; the girl's pants already ripped off and discarded; an inconsequential barrier to his lust. His final disadvantage - his back faced Harry. Even if he had not been so intent on his actions, he would have been unaware of the man in the shadows watching and judging; the last judgement the rapist would have on this earth. There would be another, of that Harry was sure, his belief unshakable, but that was for a higher authority, he merely delivered the means by which that judgement would be made; a tool in the hands of God.

The wire flicked around the attacker's neck before he registered Harry's presence; the first indication of a hell to be suffered. Harry kept the wire tight and gathered the toggles in one hand, keeping the garrotte tensioned but at the same time freeing his other arm so he could lock it around the man's neck and pull him off the terrified young woman on the ground.

At first the girl didn't respond, having retreated into the depths of her own fear; her senses diminished. Several seconds passed before she registered the man was no longer a threat. When she realised, she scrabbled away from her attacker.

"Go. Now. While you can."

She needed no second telling. Scrambling to her feet

TWENTY-THREE

she staggered into the darkness, sobbing loudly and tugging at her clothing to gain some modesty; her pants remained on the grass, abandoned in her haste to put as much distance as possible between her and this dreadful place.

She hadn't seen Harry's face. He kept the rapist between them at all times. She would only know the voice, and in her state she wouldn't be able to recall anything significant. The only face she would remember would be that of her tormentor. She would remember that for a long time to come.

The man stopped writhing and Harry slackened the garrotte a little to let him breathe again. He didn't want him to die, not just now.

He brought him back to a semi-conscious state, he didn't fancy trying to drag a dead weight deeper into the bushes, not one this size. The man had more girth than height; Humpty Dumpty in the graveyard. Give him a little hope and he would co-operate, move willingly, and if he didn't, a little tightening of the garrotte could be very persuasive.

He and Harry were going to get acquainted for a while. Harry suspected he would enjoy it far more than the disgusting creature rubbing his throat and staring up at him in confusion from the ground.

HARRY

CHAPTER TWENTY-FOUR

Not since Kuwait had Harry been on such a high. He knew he should sleep, but he couldn't; the excitement too much to contain. Another life taken; this time by choice, not necessity.

Something exists inside a living person which cannot be defined; an energy, a life-force. Harry saw the moment it left forever by watching the eyes. One moment life existed, and then it had gone, with nothing visible leaving the body. This both fascinated and excited him, but the exuberance tonight came from another source. After all these years he finally found a purpose; to rid society of people like the abhorrent creature he left in the cemetery. They didn't deserve to breathe the same air as him, nor any other decent, living, law abiding citizen.

To Harry, rape and murder amounted to the same thing. Either way a life is taken. No one ever truly recovers from rape, it becomes a life sentence; once done it cannot be undone, nor compensated for. Taking something that doesn't belong to you is never right, and if it isn't offered willingly, it doesn't belong to you. So in his

TWENTY-FOUR

own mind, what Harry did last night was not murder, but a service to society, an exorcism of the evil; doing the world and its people a favour. If more of his kind roamed the streets, crime rates would fall; fewer individuals would be willing to risk being caught and punished by someone like Harry.

By not being constrained, he would achieve what the law couldn't. The police had their hands tied, as upholders of the law they must abide by it too. What a pity the lawmakers did not see the irony of the legislation protecting the guilty as equally as the innocent. He would become judge, jury and executioner rolled into one, but would use his power wisely. Only those who slipped through the net of justice would meet his friends.

Last night had not been planned; a chance encounter on his way back from a planned one, but even so, things went surprisingly well. Undoubtedly he left traces at the scene; possibly the button missing from his coat, but that couldn't be helped. His DNA was not in any database, nor his fingerprints on file. The military records remained sealed, and the MOD would require cast iron proof of his guilt, in triplicate, before they would unseal them. So, to prove his involvement they would have to catch him first, and he did not intend to allow that to happen. Complacency caused the downfall of more than one criminal. That, and of course stupidity. Although aware he was intelligent, he did not overestimate his abilities, nor did he underestimate the police, and he would ensure he never became complacent. Future sorties would be planned to minimise his exposure, leaving as little evidence as possible, and given his lifestyle, most trace evidence could be explained away.

Considering the spur of the moment action, he considered the Bible reference to be a stroke of genius. He wondered how long it would be before someone worked out what the numbers and letters meant. He doubted any of the local cops would know the scriptures as well as he. Of course, there would be times when he would still have to improvise, but now aware of his purpose he would plan a little better. He would continue leaving clues to the purpose for the killing. That was only fair. He did not want the police to think these attacks were random. He wanted them to know he was on their side, that he understood their frustration of having to abide by the laws they upheld. He would be the force they longed to be.

Living by himself in the flat meant he could come and go as he pleased; no one tracked his movements, no one to answer to. His neighbours left him alone, and he did the same. Harry never had a steady woman in his life; in his youth there been many a fling but no time for anything serious. In his later years, he didn't have the inclination. He wasn't gay, but neither did he crave the company of the opposite sex. None of them ever came close to being pack members. He didn't choose to be that way, it was just the way things were, and over the years Harry became content with his own company. He did enjoy the companionship of others when he chose the companions, but his flat was his cave, and for him alone. His way of living gave him the perfect situation for his new role. He would roam the streets looking for his next victim, then return to his sanctuary to plan their demise.

CHAPTER TWENTY-FIVE

Each connection hidden from the last and bouncing around the world via VPN after VPN, 0rchid felt she was ready to make the attempt.

Throughout school she felt comfortable around computers, as if they were friends. She showed a tremendous aptitude for programming and developing hardware, but it was never a career choice for her. This was a hobby, a means to relax; although if asked about her present state of mind, relaxed would undoubtedly be one of the words excluded from her answer.

Her day job didn't challenge her but this certainly did and more than made up for the lack of excitement in her employment. A few more safeguards to put in place and she would be ready to make the attempt.

There; now if anyone detected the intrusion, the trace would go back to a computer somewhere in Moscow. Judging from the speed of the connection it more than likely belonged to a business rather than an individual, but this was hardly relevant; no one from the UK would be going there to challenge the owner, and she could hardly

TWENTY-FIVE

see the Russian authorities falling over themselves to help the British.

'Okay, show time.' She probed the usual methods of gaining entry and got the responses she expected. The ports were blocked and monitored. She wasn't looking for a way in here, but wanted to test the responses to her intrusion attempts. If she managed to get inside the system she needed to know if the intrusion had been detected. They may have methods she wasn't aware of but there was nothing she could do about that, other than walk away right now, and that wasn't going to happen.

She set the software on its task in the same locations and this time, the intrusion attempts produced no response. She still couldn't access the system yet, but at least she could now set the rest of the software on the task of finding a vulnerability without fear of the system detecting the attempt. This might just work.

She let the computer do its thing while she made herself a cup of tea. No sense in sitting in front of the monitor waiting for something to happen; the computer would tell her when it gained entry.

She was on her third tea and half way through her book when a quiet ping alerted her attention. She stared at the screen. Whilst she knew in theory she should be able to do this, she also knew the gap between theory and practice could often be a large one. Her heart beat faster; what she saw now told her she'd built the mother of all bridges.

As a child her parents took her on a trip to Stump Cross Caverns in Yorkshire. The coloured lights turned the natural features into a fairy wonderland for a nine-year old, the memory made all the more poignant as that turned out to be the last holiday they had together. Now that same nine-year old, still inside her head, gazed in wonderment at the information on her screen. A fairy grotto for an extraordinary hacker.

She checked the connection and saw no change in the

activity from the servers. She hadn't tripped any security measures as far as she could tell. She achieved the impossible.

0rchid burst into tears. Whether the emotion of the moment or the thought of her parents had overwhelmed her, she couldn't be sure; probably the combination. She missed her parents terribly, even after so many years.

She took a deep breath, wiped away her tears, blew her nose then set about exploring this Aladdin's Cave of information and with access to all the files as a super administrator, what a treasure trove it would be.

CHAPTER TWENTY-SIX

"The victim, according to the ID found on the body, is thirty-five-year-old, Ronald Henry Silver, a British citizen, and not in the system. He was found yesterday morning in Tower Hamlets' Cemetery Park, by a dog walker. As you can see from the photographs his trousers were around his ankles and his genitalia had been removed and forced into his mouth. Ligature marks around the neck indicate some form of strangulation, but the cause of death appears to be asphyxiation from his own body parts. So the mutilation was ante mortem."

Around the table the officers studied the photographs intently, male officers trying not to dwell on the thought of having their 'bits' cut off while still alive, or indeed at all; legs crossing and uncrossing as the thought wormed its way in anyway.

In addition to the existing caseload, the team now had to deal with this. Besides the murder of Brian Hamilton, they were currently working on a series of rapes, recently handed to them by the Sapphire Team. Three domestic murders completed the list of outstanding investigations. In those cases, the attacker was known to the victim.

TWENTY-SIX

This one didn't fit the mould. The sadism involved suggested someone either with a deep personal grudge against the individual, or mental instability. Some would argue that anyone committing a murder must be mentally unstable in the first place. Not always the case in Helene's experience. Either way, this murder was sadistic, brutal and without compassion. The perpetrator went out of their way to inflict pain and suffering. The case would go to the top of the pile, and although there were a lot of politics involved around the death of the homeless man; politics from some senior figures in the government; a former serviceman was dead after all, and they didn't want the public to think the government didn't care. The sheer brutality meant this case would take precedence. A smaller number of officers would continue on the murder of Hamilton, but at the moment a lack of leads hampered the case.

DCI Mackay continued. "A letter followed by four numbers has been carved into the left thigh, probably by the same implement used to remove the genitalia. The significance of these isn't yet known. According to the Pathologist, the weapon used is surgically sharp. No weapons have been found in the vicinity to date. Other items have been recovered from the scene, including what appears to be a coat button. It doesn't match anything the victim wore and at the moment we cannot assume it came from the perpetrator either. We'll keep an open mind; the cemetery is used on occasion for various purposes other than burying bodies. Hairs found on the victim suggest he came into contact with someone shortly before his death. Whether that is relevant remains to be seen. DNA from the hairs and the button is being processed as we speak. Your thoughts please, boys and girls?"

Helene looked along the table, wondering who the first would be to speak. DS Barnes usually stepped in straight away, and always to the point. She had high hopes for him and considered him an extremely valuable member of the team. She valued all the members, or they wouldn't be there. There would be no one along for the ride on her team. A member not pulling their weight found themselves out before they could mutter an excuse, and her word was final.

Barnes stayed unusually quiet this morning, and it was DC Murray who broke the silence.

"Anything taken, money credit cards, etcetera?"

"His wallet contained thirty-five pounds in cash, a number of credit cards and a rail pass. He still had his watch on. At the moment I'm not thinking a robbery gone wrong for a motive, and even if it turns out to be one, why the mutilation?"

"Maybe he'd been caught with his pants down in the wrong place, Ma'am. A jealous husband getting his revenge?"

Helene nodded. "He certainly had his pants down. Maybe it could be a revenge attack, Karen, but why choose the cemetery?"

"Opportunity maybe, right place an...."

"I think he's a rapist, Ma'am," Barnes interrupted. "Sorry, Karen."

The officer inclined her head in acknowledgement of his apology and motioned for him to continue.

Helene cocked her head to one side. "Go on, Davy. What makes you think that?"

Barnes held up the photograph showing the figures carved into the thigh, D2225.

"If you look carefully, Ma'am, you can see there are two dots between the third and fourth characters." He pointed to the place on the photograph. "That makes it D22:25. If I'm right, it's from the bible, Ma'am, Deuteronomy 22 verse 25, 'But if out in the country a man

TWENTY-SIX

happens to meet a young woman pledged to be married and rapes her, only the man who has done this shall die'."

Helene held her gaze on him and shook her head.

"You're not just a pretty face are you? How the hell did you come up with that off the top of your head?"

Barnes snorted.

"When you've sat through as many sermons as I have, Ma'am, you'd remember them too. My dad's a vicar."

A ripple of laughter spread around the table and Barnes pulled a face.

"Is it any wonder I became a Jedi?"

The ripple turned into a roar. Other members of the team secretly called him the Jedi Master, alluding to his love of all things Star Wars, and his uncanny ability to spot something the others overlooked; almost as if he had been led to it. And here he was telling them in a roundabout way he knew. Nothing much got past Sergeant Barnes.

Helene smiled.

"The force is strong in this one."

That brought another round of laughter and Helene held up her hands to calm things down as Barnes threatened the others with his light sabre that doubled as a ruler. Even under an abnormal workload, morale remained high and Helene was thankful for it. It made her job easier than it might have been under the circumstances.

Order restored, the discussion turned to a plan of action for locating possible witnesses. Barnes was tasked with discovering if any other murders, recent or otherwise had the same MO of carving bible passages into the victim's skin.

Helene returned to her office. She was feeling the strain: another night with little sleep. Despite the support from her team, she still felt pressure from the job and her way of dealing with it was to find a willing and able young man to take her mind off it for a while. She was just letting off steam, or so she kept telling herself, but it must stop.

Two high profile murders, six rapes and three other murder enquiries were quite enough to deal with for now.

CHAPTER TWENTY-SEVEN

Emma glanced across to the man sitting on her right as she made her daily journey to work. As many commuters did, the man buried his head in a newspaper, isolating himself in his own little world to which other commuters were not invited.

Even though she knew it was wrong, she was not averse to reading over people's shoulders, and the story that grabbed her attention was about the body of a man found in Tower Hamlets Cemetery Park. Emma struggled to read the details with the train rattling around like this, but she thought it said the man had been murdered.

What stood out for her was the body had been found Saturday morning, the morning after she missed her stop and took the shortcut. She would find her own copy of the Metro when she got off the train and read the story without straining to see the details.

Twenty minutes later she needed to find somewhere to sit. She felt sick. The police report gave scant detail other than it was being treated as a murder. Someone had been murdered the same night Emma cut through the park. The scream she thought she heard could be connected to this

TWENTY-SEVEN

man's death, and she walked through the same park, at the same time. It could easily have been her. Despite the unseasonably high temperatures, Emma felt cold.

She checked her watch. As usual she was in plenty of time for work and would normally reach her desk at least thirty minutes early, allowing her to ease into the day, rather than the need to hit the ground running. With a dry mouth and shaking hands, she entered the Starbucks close to her office and ordered a latte. At her table she struggled not to spill the drink as she read over the story again.

She must tell someone about the scream. Even though she saw nothing, the fact she heard something might be the missing piece of information that would allow the police to find the killer.

With her smartphone, she took a photograph of the bottom of the article; an appeal for information carrying both the Crimestoppers and local police telephone numbers. Emma left the paper on the table with her half-finished coffee and dashed to work. She arrived in the office with minutes to spare, an unusual occurrence and commented upon by more than one of her colleagues. She smiled politely, blamed the tube, and booted up her computer, resolving to give one of those numbers a call at her first break.

CHAPTER TWENTY-EIGHT

Colin Worthing had known little other than violence in his life. The modern term for his upbringing would be 'from a dysfunctional home', but in reality that could apply to most of the homes on the estate where he grew up. While few of the other kids stayed out of trouble completely, none sought it with the same fervour as he. Some would say it was inevitable, given the background, but others would argue that not everyone with a violent childhood turns out to be monsters themselves, and the term 'monster' fitted Worthing like a glove.

His partner in crime, and the brains of the operation, was an associate by the name of Morgan. Aside from Morgan's legitimate business in light engineering, he had fingers in loan sharking and protection rackets. Those proved to be more lucrative than the workshop, leading Morgan to turn his hand to any number of illegal activities as opportunities arose. As was fitting for the brains of the operation he took the lion's share of the proceeds, but Worthing still received handsome compensation, particularly as he supplied little more than muscle and occasionally acted as a mule. Morgan understood the

TWENTY-EIGHT

value of a trustworthy minder, and Worthing fitted the bill exactly. He had no qualms about getting physical with people; breaking fingers, arms, legs, and if the occasion called for it, the odd neck or two. In short, Colin Worthing was the sort of person you wouldn't merely cross the street to avoid, you would seek a new postcode.

A regular visitor to the gym, Worthing's physique was that of some of the more competitive body builders. His shoulders merged into his head without any visible form of neck and the girth of his upper arms would rival the average person's thighs. Not only did the term monster fit his demeanour but equally it could be applied to his physical presence. In short, Worthing was a force to be reckoned with.

Today was collection day for this area, and the bag man, Worthing, picked up the protection money from various premises on Burdett Road. Not all the shops were targeted, only those whose owners would be easy to intimidate, independents and especially the elderly. Never the Chinese; you never knew their affiliation. Crossing one of the Triads was a bad idea, both for business and reasons of personal safety.

"Where's the rest of it? This can't be more than a ton." Worthing riffled the small wad of notes.

"I've told you, that is all I can afford this week." An air of defiance emanated from the old Bangladeshi newsagent as he stood behind the till.

"I don't give a shit what you can afford, you pay what we say or suffer the consequences, understand?"

The man shook his head.

"I just do not have it to give you. You have to understand, some weeks are better than others and sometimes I just cannot..."

He never got to finish his sentence. Worthing reached over the counter, grabbed hold of the newsagent by the ears and dragged him onto the counter top. He bunched what little hair still grew on the man's head into his hand, yanked his head back and smashed it into the counter; the explosion of blood and crunch of bone a sure sign the old newsagent's nose had been shattered.

"I'll be back tomorrow, and you better have it all or else things will get far worse for you, my friend. Understand? Far worse." He flung the cash into the air as he turned away.

Leaving the man sprawled on the counter top, five pound notes fluttering around him, Worthing strolled out of the shop, picking up a chocolate bar on the way. There were days when he loved his job, and this was one of them.

ooOoo

The Old Man didn't venture this way too often, preferring to stay around the Bow and Stratford areas, but last night's sleeping place brought him close to the neighbourhood. Whilst in the vicinity he thought he would venture down to Duke Street Wharf, on the banks of the Thames, and see if the lads there had heard of any attacks. Things had gone quiet around Bow and he wondered if the culprits decided to move to a new area after Brian died.

His thoughts were interrupted as someone barged into his shoulder from behind. Not a word of apology, nor even an acknowledgment of his existence. The Old Man opened his mouth to say something as the man tossed a chocolate wrapper onto the ground and continued on his way.

A wail of pain from behind him grabbed his attention before he could utter a word to the ignorant oaf he had just encountered. He turned back in time to see an old Asian man stagger out of the shop, his face covered in blood; one hand clutched his nose, the other alternated between

TWENTY-EIGHT

waving about wildly and the back of it being slapped against his forehead in a dramatic gesture of stress. He collapsed against the shop front, slid to the floor, and came to rest by the open shop doorway. The Old Man shuffled over to see if there was anything he could do to help.

As he squatted down to speak, the man who had bumped into him called from along the street.

"I'll be back tomorrow, have it ready, or else."

The Old Man watched as he threaded his way through the traffic waiting at the lights, before disappearing from sight behind a line of vehicles.

This is getting to be a habit, he thought, as he dialled 999 from the call box a few yards away from where the newsagent lay slumped on the pavement.

A crowd gathered and several people were now tending to the injured shop keeper, so the Old Man made his way across the road to the bus stop. He would wait here until the ambulance arrived. After that he would continue his journey to the boys at the river, now with another question in mind about protection rackets in the area.

He remained watching until the ambulance took the old shopkeeper away, before shuffling off in the direction of the wharf.

A figure detached itself from the shadow of the nearby bushes and followed a respectable distance behind.

CHAPTER TWENTY-NINE

Harry thoroughly enjoyed this part. Of course he enjoyed killing even more, but it was this that made it so special; getting to know his victims, their routines, habits, who they saw and what they did. Thank goodness, so far none of them had their own transport or he wouldn't have been able to keep up the surveillance; one advantage of living in London was so many people relied on the public transport network.

Sometimes it was as simple as being in the right place at the right time to keep an eye on the intended victim. At others, he followed the person from place to place, gathering his information. On occasion he found himself dressed inappropriately for a given location and he would break off the surveillance; only to return another day if necessary, and more suitable dressed. He never viewed an obstacle as a setback; each he treated as another learning opportunity, a chance to fine tune the whole operation.

Operation: now there was a word he hadn't been involved with for a while, but that is what this had become. Harry understood the value of planning; any operation could rapidly turn to disaster without planning.

TWENTY-NINE

The British Armed forces were well aware and made sure their troops were too. Operation Deadwood, that's an appropriate name for it, he thought. He often wondered about the names they chose for operations. They were supposed to be unrelated to the operation itself, so how did Desert Storm get through? Other were totally unrelated but he had to wonder who sat there and picked them. On this occasion, he did, and he didn't care if it was related to what he was doing because it was only in his head. Until the day someone invented a way to read people's thoughts it was the safest place to store anything.

He kept everything in his head, preferring never to take notes. Notes can be used against if you are captured and in Civvy Street they can be used against you in a court of law. He did not intend to give anyone material with which to prosecute him. His ability to remember extraordinary detail showed from an early age. Harry's IQ put him in the 'highly gifted' category; this alone would not explain his exceptional gift to recall the smallest of details, but had he been subjected to the psychological tests now, more sophisticated than the ones he took when selected for SBS training, they would perhaps have identified Harry as being on the autistic spectrum and his memory feats being that of a savant. Harry didn't care how he got his abilities, he knew he had them, and how to use them, that was all that mattered.

Not only did Harry attend the meeting in the pub, he also ventured along to one of Leslie's open air events, as part of his research into his subject. He took care to stay well out of sight. Leslie spouted the same old rhetoric about how the immigrants were dragging down the country, and only white Anglo-Saxons should be allowed to remain in this green and pleasant land. Harry wondered if it applied to immigrants from former penal colonies, or would that somehow be overlooked if Leslie got his way; Harry suspected it might. It was usual for the far right to overlook something inconvenient to their cause; Hitler wasn't blond, Goebbels hardly a giant and Goering not exactly slimmer of the year, but this did not deter the promotion of the Nordic Aryan master race, by the Nazis.

Far from blaming immigration, Harry believed the real problem lay with greedy corporations and individuals. Manufacturing processes moved overseas to save a bob or two, resulting in the country no longer producing goods of its own. Then came the rise of the service industries, creating an employment boom, but now even that had been shipped overseas, in the interests of another ounce of profit. Profit for whom? Not the average man in the street who was trying to make ends meet, nor the little old lady who couldn't afford to heat her house in the winter. No - profit for a minority who already had more wealth than they could possibly need and yet they seemed compelled to squeeze even more out of the ordinary people; the ones who just wanted to go about living their ordinary lives.

Unfortunately, there was nothing he could do about it, not yet anyway, and maybe never, but he certainly wouldn't mind removing one or two of those from the face of the earth. Let's see their fortunes help them when they are dead.

He settled down to watch the pub entrance. If all went to plan, and he saw no reason why it shouldn't, this particular brand of scum would leave shortly after eleven, and make his way through the park. How appropriate: Mr Leslie would end his life not too far from where he taken it on himself to give the Asian lad a thorough kicking.

There he was, right on cue. Leslie was nothing if not punctual; most definitely a man of routine, and tonight proved to be no exception, only this time Harry intended to break that routine for him, along with Andrew Leslie himself.

This one would be particularly enjoyable. Although Harry didn't care too much for the rest of humanity other than members of his pack, he cared even less for injustice and anyone who preached hate in such a way it would promote injustice. Andrew Leslie was just the sort of bigoted individual who fell into that category. How can the colour of someone's skin determine whether they should be allowed to live a normal life? Why not pick on the colour of their eyes, or hair, or whether they have freckles? All were equally ludicrous in Harry's mind. We are all humans, living on the same insignificant planet, orbiting around an equally insignificant star, and yet all we do is squabble amongst ourselves. No wonder the aliens leave us alone. They haven't been able to figure us out yet.

To an outsider this would appear to be incongruous with Harry's view on membership of his pack, but it was in keeping with many psychological studies where the level of loyalty was determined by the nature of the threat. Villagers may not like members of the next village, but if threatened by another country they would fight to defend their neighbours. Harry expanded his definition of pack membership quite readily if he felt someone needed his protection, or more importantly, if they deserved it.

This man deserved something else, and tonight he would be rewarded. Leslie stepped out of the pub doorway, paused for a moment, cupped his hands and lit the cigarette already bobbing between his lips, then took a long drag, exhaling the smoke upwards into the night air, curling away like a departing soul; how apt, Harry thought. Leslie waved towards of one of his cronies who said goodnight and the leader of BARE set off towards the park.

For a moment Harry wondered why he didn't drink in a pub closer to his home. Perhaps this one tolerated the extremist views spouted by this moron, or maybe he had been barred from all the rest. He would look into that sometime. There may be others who deserved his attention.

Already in front of Leslie, Harry moved as quickly as

he dared without attracting unwanted attention, in order to get into place in the park. Safely hidden, Harry knew he would not have long to wait, and sure enough the figure of Leslie appeared right on cue.

Leslie was not aware of Harry's presence until the garrotte looped over his neck. Exerting the right amount of pressure caused Leslie to pass out in a matter of seconds, and Harry swiftly dragged him from the path deep into the bushes. He wanted to spend some time with this one. He would know he was being killed, and he would know why, Harry intended to make absolutely sure of that.

CHAPTER THIRTY

Helene trawled through the mountain of paperwork on her desk. Forensic reports on the rapes concluded seminal fluid from the same person was present in all the attacks. Bad enough having a serial rapist in the first case, but for one to be active now, they needed that like another hole in the head. Of course, the database did not show a match for the DNA, they could not be that lucky. How handy would it be if everyone's DNA profile was on record, but that smacked too much of 'big brother'.

Both of the domestic murder cases appeared to be open and shut; fingerprints from the spouses found on the murder weapons, the victim's blood on their clothing, a long history of violence towards the partner, and in one of the cases, a confession. It was all too easy to become complacent even with overwhelming evidence. A good lawyer would argue the evidence to be circumstantial, dismissing every piece with a perfectly believable explanation, to the point where the jury had sufficient reasonable doubt to acquit. Helene had seen it happen before and was determined for it not to happen on her watch. One of the suspects refused to talk; the lawyer

THIRTY

advising 'no comment' to every question. They would need to dig deeper to find the one piece of evidence that couldn't be dismissed. It was there somewhere; it always was; just a matter of finding it.

She didn't mind the admin; this was the important stuff. Somewhere in here lay the 'the smoking gun' as her cousins across the Atlantic liked to say.

Helene spent some time on an exchange program with West Palm Beach Homicide Unit in Florida. Although many considered Florida to be a dream posting, especially in the springtime, the reality turned out to be quite different. Some of the West Palm Beach neighbourhood crime rates exceeded the national average, especially for homicides. She discovered the work to be akin to Henry Ford's production line; as one case ended another started, with several going on in-between. Helene thoroughly enjoyed the experience, and came back with fresh ideas and new techniques, which was the whole purpose of the exchange program. Conversely, the West Palm Beach detective assigned to the Met Police returned to Florida convinced the average British bobby was completely stark raving bonkers going up against hardened criminals, armed with nothing more than a metal stick and a can of pepper spray. The American felt naked without his Smith and Wesson .40. He took his hat off the British Police for remaining one of the few forces in the world not to routinely carry guns.

Helene thought it sad these particular murders in front of her were committed by people who once professed love for the murdered person. She doubted if any of them knew what the word meant; not even sure of it herself, not since...she paused, she promised not to let herself go there again.

Helene refocused on the job in hand. Her 'To be Actioned' tray didn't just overflow, it created an archipelago of paper islands on the carpet tiles. None of that paperwork lying on the floor related to nicking real villains as far as she was concerned. Home Office requests for statistic, reports, evaluations, explanations - the list went on, as if they didn't have enough on their plates without satisfying some faceless statistician. She failed to see how an onslaught of requests would enable the Police to improve crime rates. The majority of information collected would be entered into a computer somewhere, ignored for several years, and eventually consigned to the archives to be forgotten for evermore; statistics for the sake of them. Every Home Secretary brought a new way of doing things, required more reports, and all the while cutting budgets. Most of the officers she worked with thought they had been doing so much with so little for so long, they now were qualified to do Anything with Nothing. Just as long as Whitehall got the stats, everything would be fine. Form filling or feeling collars was what it boiled down to; give her the latter any day.

A knock on the door brought her back from her internal rant. DS Barnes popped his head through the door.

"Yes, Davy?"

"I thought you'd want to hear this right away, Ma'am. We've got a match on the DNA from the body in the cemetery." He stopped and put on his boyish grin.

"Don't make me wait, Davy, or I'll tear something off you, and you won't like it."

"It's the rapist, Ma'am, the one we've been looking for." He couldn't help but smile.

"How certain?"

"The DNA is 1 in twenty-million, but we also got fibre and hair match too."

Both of the officers understood the dangers of assuming a one in twenty-million match meant the odds of someone else being the perpetrator were twenty-

THIRTY

million to one. The statistics were far more complex than that, but in this case the odds swung dramatically in their favour boosted by the additional evidence.

Helen put her hands on her head, closed her eyes and threw her head back. She stayed that way for a few moments before looking at Barnes.

"Brilliant, Davy. That's the best news we've had all week, month even. All we need to do now is find out who killed him."

She tilted her head on one side. "You know, I'm not that sure I want to do that."

"Ma'am?"

She shook her head.

"Never mind. I'm thinking out loud. Right, we better start wrapping up the rape enquiries. Anything on a similar MO?"

DS Barnes compressed his lips.

"Not a dicky bird, Ma'am. I could have sworn there would be something similar elsewhere, but nothing I can find. Looks like we have a nutter with a new idea on our hands."

"We can always make room for another nutter. Okay, keep at it, and keep me up to speed."

"Yes Ma'am."

"Oh, and Davy, well done."

DS Barnes closed the door still with a grin on his face.

Helene went back to the papers in front of her, but her mind was elsewhere. Did they have some sort of vigilante on their hands? Did this man's killer really know he was the rapist, and if so, how did he know? Was this just coincidence? Had he known him? A multitude of questions swirled around in her head, but one kept popping back to the top. Did she really want to catch the man who caught and punished a serial rapist in the most brutal yet fitting way possible? She was alarmed she thought that way, but she saw too many evil people literally get away with murder. Perhaps the time had come to bring some justice back into the world, even the rough variety.

CHAPTER THIRTY-ONE

This killing would give even greater pleasure than the others. Harry did not like bullies, he proved that as a child, and this man was a bully of the greatest magnitude. Since he uncovered the scam, he spent three weeks observing Worthing and learned he worked as a minder for a low grade crook by the name of Morgan; only the two of them were involved in the protection racket.

Morgan appeared to be something of an Arthur Daley character; fingers in all sorts of pies, some legitimate, most of them not. Unlike Daley, Morgan was no lovable rogue, but a nasty piece of work. Harry quickly established Morgan and Worthing worked to a set routine, not very wise for people on the fringes of the law or handling substantial amounts of cash. Worthing collected the protection money from different areas over a three-day period each week; always the same day in each area. At the end of each day he returned to the railway-arch lock-up in Mill Place; nothing on the wall or gate to the premises indicated what type of business operated from there.

Harry believed Worthing came here to hand over the

THIRTY-ONE

dosh to Morgan, because shortly after he would leave the lock-up and disappear in his Jaguar XJS. Harry surmised he would be taking the cash to a night safe in one of the nearby banks, while Worthing always remained behind for an hour to do who knows what? Harry never got close enough to take a peek inside. That would have been far too risky. He did not want to give himself away at this stage of the game. Harry noted Worthing's regular pattern to lock up the workshop, stroll to the main road just in time to catch the number 115 bus, get off six stops later and take the short walk to his flat in Nelson Street. Harry considered taking on Worthing at his apartment, but soon dismissed the thought. Council flats were not noted for their extra thick walls, and Harry suspected there may be a certain amount of noise involved in his plans. No, the workshop was far more isolated and suitable for this operation.

Harry harboured no real concerns over what Worthing did in that final hour in the workshop, he would have the element of surprise. Even if Worthing saw him coming, he wouldn't be expecting Harry to be a threat. He would make sure of it. Worthing might be a thug, but Harry had no doubt his own training would be far superior to anything Worthing may have undertaken, if indeed he'd been trained at all. He might be a body builder but that didn't make him a fighter and Harry knew how to fight, especially the dirty kind. In Harry's mind, both Worthing and Morgan were rank amateurs; not once in the three weeks had Worthing done anything that looked remotely like a counter-surveillance move. Whether that was cockiness or ignorance, Harry was unsure, he suspected it might be a bit of both.

The short nights presented a small problem. Harry would prefer to enter the premises under the cover of darkness; less likelihood of being seen by witnesses, but as it wasn't in his control, he didn't fret about it. Concentrate on the things he could control and always make an exit strategy in case if it all went wrong; that was the only way to plan.

Harry slipped quietly through the wicket door in the outside gate and entered the yard. The double doors to the workshop were slightly ajar, not sufficient for him to see inside and angled in such a way that anyone inside would not be able to see Harry enter the yard; another amateur mistake. The sound of machinery reached Harry's ears. He peered cautiously around the edge of the doorway. A quick glance told him all he needed to know. The premises contained a small machine shop. Worthing stood with his back to Harry and appeared to be turning something on a lathe. Perhaps this was one of Morgan's legitimate businesses and maybe Worthing was a skilled turner or something. Harry would be able to ask him soon enough.

He eased the door open sufficiently wide for him to slip inside; he had no concerns about the noise; Worthing stood next to a working lathe, he would not hear a creaky door.

Harry's fingers curled around the wooden toggles, once again seeking solace in the familiarity of their shape. His breathing slowed and his mind cleared. Like a cat preparing to pounce on a bird, Harry's focus remained firmly on his target. It was time for his friend to get to work.

ooOoo

Harry felt a small pang of regret. Overwhelming Worthing had been far easier than anticipated and he had done so long before Worthing registered Harry's presence in the workshop. There had been no challenge involved in overcoming this brute of a man. And brute he was. He clearly worked out, but his muscles were no match for a highly trained soldier with a garrotte. Harry had hoped for a bit more resistance, a chance to humiliate this giant, but

THIRTY-ONE

not to worry, there would be plenty of time for them to get acquainted.

Conveniently for Harry, the shop contained a small hoist consisting of a chain operated block and tackle suspended from a metal beam set into the sides of the arch; presumably installed to lift the heavier pieces onto the nearby milling machine. The human piece dangling from it now could certainly be classed as heavy, but its organic nature made it unsuitable to be milled. The thought crossed Harry's mind for a moment but he had something far better in mind for this bully.

Harry bound Worthing's hands together and to the hook on the hoist. He lifted him high enough for only his toes to be touching the ground, his ankles he tied to a length of wood to keep his legs apart. He inserted a large wad of rag between his teeth, and kept in place by another tied over his nose and mouth, making him look like a bank robber in a spaghetti western. Then Harry waited.

When Worthing came round, and despite his precarious position, he flashed anger from his eyes. He could do little else being bound and gagged. He seemed oblivious to the fact he was naked. Harry had no doubts were the man free he would be attempting to kill him, but he was hardly in a position to do so.

He moved closer to the writhing man, and whispered in his ear, gently tapping him on the side of his head with an iron bar.

"I know you like to knock people around, Mr Worthing, especially those who are unable to defend themselves. So I thought I would give you a little lesson in pain and anger management, and perhaps it will serve as a big lesson for those who will hear about it. I don't like bullies, I never have. Of course, this is not for my benefit you understand, but I do it on behalf of all those you have hurt over the years. Unfortunately, you won't be able to apologise to them for the error of your ways. Oh no, it's far too late for that."

Harry looked into Worthing's eyes and was rewarded with the first flicker of fear. Only now did this man realise he was about to die. Until that moment he believed he would somehow escape the situation. How much he was going to suffer, he had no idea, but Harry knew; in the minutest detail he knew the amount of pain he would inflict on him.

"Now where shall we start? Maybe your toes, or perhaps your fingers." Harry left the words dangling before whispering, "I know, we'll start with the ribs."

And with that he swung the iron bar between Worthing's legs and into his crotch. The intense pain caused him to involuntarily lift his knees bringing his full weight on his arms, that's when Harry delivered his second blow, shattering both the radius and ulna in the man's right arm. Worthing dangled from the hook with one broken and one undamaged arm.

An adult human contains two hundred and six bones. Harry broke two of them with one blow, but he didn't want to rush things, this would be a long, and for Harry, such a pleasurable night.

CHAPTER THIRTY-TWO

"So, what you think, man?"

"I dunno, bro. It's not like I know you proper, man, innit."

Smoke rolled his eyes and shook his head.

"C'mon man, you've known me and her for over a year now. What you think we are, the filth? Pull the hair, man. It ain't no wig; the tats don't wash off, see?"

To prove the point Smoke wet his finger and vigorously rubbed the skull tattoo on his left arm.

Anyone even so much as glancing at Smoke and his girlfriend, Gypsy, would know them for what they were; bikers. Not the weekend warriors clad in the latest team leathers pretending to be Rossi, Marquez or Lorenzo. These belonged to the one percenters, the outlaws, the biker gangs. Or rather they would be one percenters if they belonged to any of the MCs. They wore no colours and swore allegiance to no one. Smoke and Gypsy were lone riders, independents.

"Look, man. I'm telling ya, my mate has his hands on

CHAPTER THIRTY-THREE

Two months had passed since that morning Jakey came to the flat with news of the old tramp's death. As Grease predicted, the police investigation ground to a halt with no viable leads. Regular appeals appeared in the local paper and even on the TV, but it seemed no one witnessed anything and there was even confusion as to whether the attacks had been carried out by one or two people. Grease hadn't the slightest doubt they would remain in the clear.

The joinery company they worked for produced doors and window frames, but would make the odd staircase when asked to do so. Both of the lads, being skilled, time-served carpenters, could turn their hand to any job in the workshop. Neither gave their supervisor as much as a hint of being trouble, although he noticed they were being a bit cool with each other. That was since the factory had closed for an extra day to allow some new machinery to be installed. He didn't care too much about their personal differences as long they got on with their work, and they did. Even the owner, a grumpy old man at the best of times, wished he employed more like them. They would go the extra mile to get an order out in time. Good, solid,

THIRTY-THREE

hardworking lads, he couldn't ask for more.

Grease knew they would be fine; why shouldn't they be with the reputation they'd earned? No one expected the steady guys to be trouble. That was reserved for the stereotypes, the unemployed, the skinheads, the heavily tattooed, not the 9-5, hardworking, clean-cut lads. People should know better; remember Clockwork Orange?

Grease spent plenty of time thinking this through. They disposed of anything incriminating from that night. The clothing and shoes placed into bins nowhere near the scene or their houses; the baseball bat dropped into the Thames. No sense in giving it to the filth on a plate was there? Trainers and clothing of different brands replaced the ones used on that night and the shiny, new baseball bat, made of aluminium, replaced the wooden one; everything purchased from another area. He doubted the police kept an eye on that sort of thing, but he would take no chances.

Grease was bright, he thought ahead and planned, and he knew Jakey would see sense eventually. He hoped it would be soon, he felt the need to go and brighten up his evenings once again, ridding the borough of what he considered to be the fleas of the neighbourhood.

Apparently they weren't the only ones on a crusade. The local papers all carried the story about the rapist who'd been found dead in the cemetery with his bits cut off and rammed down his throat. Well, he couldn't say he would lose any sleep over that, and he had to admit the method of the man's death had a touch of genius about it. It was about time people got together to clean up the area. The rozzers weren't doing anything about it; they seemed to be more intent on nicking people for having a joint, than tracking down the real villains.

As Grease finalised the assembly of a large oak door for an old Edwardian house, Jakey stopped in front of him with a piece of moulding for a window frame.

"You were right, Grease."

Grease gave him a look of 'Of course I'm right.'
Jakey returned him a sheepish grin.

"Maccies?" Grease asked.

The forty-minute lunch break would give them adequate time to nip up the road to the nearest McDonald's. Grease would have preferred a flame grilled BK, but beggars can't be choosers; the nearest BK just a bit too far for a lunch break.

Jakey waited a moment before nodding his agreement and going back to his window frame.

ooOoo

As Grease and Jakey discussed what to do next in the churchyard of St Mary's-atte-Bow, Grease sensed he had calmed down enough to consider going back on their night time crusades. He knew he would. After much discussion they agreed on an outing the following Friday night. They were still discussing the details when a scruffy old man shuffled through the gate. Grease tapped Jakey on the arm and nodded his head towards the tramp.

"There's the reason we need to keep this up. Persuade losers like him to move somewhere else."

The man plopped himself down on the bench opposite without giving them so much as a glance. He pulled a crumpled paper bag from inside his coat and inspected the contents. He extracted what appeared to be a half-eaten sausage roll and attacked it with some degree of enthusiasm.

"Gawd, that's disgusting," muttered Grease.

The old man paused his chewing, looked up as if noticing them for the first time, studied each of them in turn, raised his eyebrows, returned his eyes to his sausage roll and started munching again.

"Got a problem, boys?" he said while still chewing,

THIRTY-THREE

bits of pastry scattering from his lips like leaves from an autumn tree, alighting in the undergrowth of the beard below.

Grease wrinkled his nose as if smelling something unpleasant.

"You could say that. Why don't you go somewhere else?"

The tramp continued chewing while giving the question some thought. He stopped chewing only long enough to utter one word.

"Why?"

Grease hadn't expected to be answered back but didn't see any reason to back down.

"Because you make the place look untidy, that's why."

The man flicked his head upwards and raised his eyebrows as if saying 'I see', while continuing to chomp away. He stopped eating and stabbed the sausage roll towards them, emphasising his words.

"If you think I make it untidy now, sonny, you should see when I'm sleeping here. Papers everywhere, and I snore something terrible. Why don't you come back one night and have a gander, or do churchyards make you scared...little boy?" The last two words spoken slowly in a low tone.

He went back to consuming his food.

Grease held his anger in check. Now was not the time, certainly not in broad daylight and with many people around, but he made a mental note this might well be the place. He would bear it in mind, though the proximity to the main road made things a little too public to be completely comfortable with the idea. Still, in the early hours of the morning it might work out. On the way back to work he would keep a lookout for CCTV cameras, both public and private. It wasn't unheard of to be caught out by an unlucky sighting on the footage from a private camera. A trip up here later in the week wouldn't go amiss either, can't be too careful.

He turned to his companion. "Come on, Jakey. This place has lost its appeal."

Grease rose from the bench with Jakey in tow. As they were leaving he called over his shoulder.

"Best you find somewhere else, old man. Some nasty things have been happening around here."

The old man never so much as glanced in their direction as he raised two fingers and carried on with his sausage roll.

CHAPTER THIRTY-FOUR

It had been some time since the station held a press conference of this size. Three empty chairs behind a large desk dominated one end of the room. On the desk, a forest of microphones took centre stage; a tangle of cables led away to various reporters from a variety of radio and TV stations, and those newspaper reporters preferring to embrace the new technology rather than write. The remainder of the room was filled to capacity with seated journalists, and a good number of them, tardy in their arrival, found themselves confined to jostling shoulders with others in the same boat.

It was clear to all present; the news of a possible serial killer on the streets of London swelled in the minds of both press and the public alike. Like royal weddings, dead bodies sold newspapers, and rumour had it, body number three had been discovered.

Nicky traded banter with a few colleagues, some of whom he had known for many years, while some of the younger reporters looked on wondering who he was; a few of the more knowledgeable ones recognised him and offered a deferential nod which he returned. By hard work and time served, Nicky gained the mantle of godfather of Fleet Street. Some believed he was a dinosaur, his time had been and gone, and it was time for him to move over. Invariably, they were the young pretenders, like his editor, the ones who considered his methods to be archaic, his ethics to be outdated; the ones for whom 'the people have a right to know' was a mantra justifying the means by which they gathered their news; intrusive and often illegal.

The hubbub of voices gave way to a flurry of camera shutters as the door behind the desks opened. Three people filed in; a man and two women, one of whom was the only uniformed person. The three officers took their seats; the uniformed officer starting the proceedings immediately.

"Ladies, gentlemen. Thank you for attending this afternoon. I am Assistant Commissioner Patricia Gallan. On my right is Detective Chief Superintendent Brandon, and to my left, Detective Chief Inspector Helene MacKay, Senior Investigating Officer. Chief Superintendent Brandon will make a statement and then we will take a few questions."

Brandon looked over his glasses at the throng of reporters waiting for him to start, as another round of shutters and camera flashes launched into full flow.

"At 8 a.m. this morning the body of a man was discovered in premises off Mill Place, in the district of Tower Hamlets. A preliminary post-mortem report suggests cause of death to be multiple blunt force trauma, using sufficient force to break bones. We understand this form of assault is similar to a Russian torture method called zamochit, in which every bone is broken over a period of time. At this stage we are not linking it to any Russian group or individual. However, for reasons we are not at liberty to discuss at this stage of our enquiries, we believe there may be a connection to two previous murders in the Tower Hamlets' area, all three victims being persons of interest to us, prior to their deaths. You will be aware from a previous press release of the body found in the cemetery park. This first victim did not have a criminal record, however, subsequent tests have shown him to be responsible for the recent spate of rapes. This information has only just been communicated to us."

A murmur rose from the room accompanied by another round of camera activity as the journalists reacted to this revelation.

The Assistant Commissioner waited for the noise to die down again.

"The second victim, Andrew Leslie was also known to us as a right-wing white supremacist and had been on our radar for some time. His body was discovered in Mile End Park. At the moment we are not prepared to release any further details. We will now take a limited number of questions."

A young reporter from one of the tabloids was first.

"Can you tell us why you believe this is linked to the previous murders?"

Nicky sighed and shook his head. The Chief Superintendent could not have made it any clearer, they would not disclose that information, so why waste a question attempting to elicit a response that would not be forthcoming? These were professionals, unlikely to be tripped up by a cub from the gutter press.

"As I previously stated, we are not at liberty to disclose that information at this time."

Nicky watched the DCI throughout the statement and his instincts told him she was not mourning the loss of this particular individual. After several more run-of-the-mill questions Nicky decided to weigh in.

"Detective Chief Inspector, if I may?"

DCI MacKay nodded her head in acknowledgement.

"Given the, shall we say, background of the victims, do you want to catch the culprit or would you prefer he continued cleaning up the district?"

Nicky heard a few sharp intakes of breath and some mumbled comments from his colleagues, but his attention lay focused on the DCI and her immediate reaction. Well, if you are going to ask a question, you may as well ask an awkward one.

"Mr?..."

"Rolands, Nicky Rolands."

"Mr Rolands, it is my duty as a police officer to uphold the law. That law applies to all citizens and visitors to this land. There is no telling whether these particular murders specifically targeted the victims or if they were opportunistic. Either way I will investigate them to the best of my ability."

The Assistant Commissioner and the Detective Chief Superintendent both nodded vigorously in support of the DCI's statement.

Nicky wasn't convinced.

"What are your personal feelings about what he or she is achieving?"

"My personal feelings have no bearing on the matter."

Nicky thought he spotted a moment's hesitation and continued.

"So you are admitting your personal feelings are at odds with your professional duties?"

He could see the anger rising in her face.

"Mr Rolands, I am admitting nothing of the sort. You've had my answer, now please move on."

The Assistant Commissioner intervened to stop any further questions.

"I think that will be all for now. Should any further information come to light we will of course keep you informed. In the meantime, you may obtain a copy of the press release from the press officer by the usual means. Thank you for attending and your patience."

A number of shouted questions came from reporters who missed their opportunity earlier, but the three officers were already leaving the room.

Now that was interesting, thought Nicky. In his opinion, the DCI didn't believe everything she was saying. That might be worth pursuing. One of his former colleagues approached him and patted him on the back.

"Not lost the touch then Nicky? Straight for the jugular as usual."

Nicky smiled in acknowledgement and made his way towards the door. He had some research to do. DCI MacKay may be worth a few hours of his time.

CHAPTER THIRTY-FIVE

He had seen this one around often enough. Attractive on the outside, but from all accounts, a nest of vipers on the inside. Whether she had links to organised crime, or worked independently, he didn't know, and quite frankly, he didn't care. He wasn't even sure of her nationality, other than she came from the far-east somewhere.

The only certainty; she dealt in death and misery. Why the Bobbies never caught her he couldn't even begin to guess, other than maybe they just didn't have the resources. There she was now, handing out the little packets, at a price of course; some paid cash but for others, the attractive young girls, payment would come later, once they were hooked. These weren't little bags of weed; she didn't deal in anything so mundane. She supplied the hard stuff, smack, crack, crystal meth, anything that got the customers hooked and fast. Kipling knew what he was talking about when he wrote 'the female of her species is more deadly than the male.' This particular specimen; truly a black widow, drawing people into her web, injecting her own brand of venom and casting out the husk once she finished with them.

THIRTY-FIVE

Luring young girls this way was by no means a novel method of turning them, many others worked this way, but she proved to be a particularly cruel mistress.

For a while Harry had heard stories from the homeless girls she approached and some of her former girls, now roaming the streets. Some resisted her temptation but many, enticed by the promise of a drug-fuelled escape from the misery of their real world, fell into a life of prostitution, and just when they thought they could sink no lower, 'Miss Fiona' threw them out; penniless, homeless, and without hope. They were the lucky ones. Why should she care? She considered the girls to be no more than battery hens; lay or die. Harry watched her carefully, soon the mother hen would learn what it was like to be one of her cast-off girls. Harry didn't like what she did to the youngsters. He didn't like any sort of exploitation, but picking on vulnerable youngsters stirred his anger to new levels. In ordinary circumstances he would grit his teeth and growl under his breath, but Brian's death broke down the barriers, and removed whatever moral restraints existed. He would do what he thought necessary to make the world a better place.

She turned out to be a tricky one to track down; not short of street smarts when it came to routines. The girls told him of some of her haunts but presumably she communicated with her buyers by phone; she never went to the same place at the same time two days in a row. Her mistake was using the same places at all. While the Police didn't have the time or resources to stake out all the spots she might frequent, Harry had all the time in the world to go back to the same place day after day, and finally it paid off.

Still, it hadn't been an easy ride, she clearly knew about tails; doubling back, stopping suddenly, turning around, entering a building and leaving by a different exit. Harry knew all the tricks in the book and how to avoid being seen, when following. He should do; the government spent enough money on training him over the years.

A thought came to him. How come he was still doing work for the government, shouldn't some bright copper be doing this, not him? He chuckled to himself. Is this what they classify as voluntary work then?

Despite her best efforts to throw off anyone potentially following her, she led him right to where he wanted to be; her home. And what a home it was. Clearly the drug and prostitution rackets paid well. Well enough for her to have one of the swanky apartments overlooking Limehouse Basin, with Regents Canal on one side, and Limehouse Cut on the other. Which apartment, he didn't know. He couldn't be that bold and follow her in, and a quick check of the door buzzer, didn't reveal a name anywhere close to hers. She was a wily one all right. He wouldn't take her in the apartment, too many ways to get caught, and the entry covered by CCTV. He would find somewhere more secluded, dark and without cameras; public enough in the daytime, he wanted her to be seen, but dark during the night and relatively free from passers-by. He was almost certain she would use a shortcut somewhere like that; she didn't seem the sort to be worried by dark alleyways or parks.

Now he knew where she started, he would follow her on her rounds, see all her places, and make some sense of her pattern, if she had one. Most people did. Maybe she had her favourite path, or perhaps she went to the same place on a particular day and only the timings varied. Whatever it was, she would make a mistake, and Harry would be there and take the opportunity to rid the borough of another nasty piece of work, and a waste of oxygen.

ooOoo

A week of following 'Miss Fiona' revealed a fatal flaw in her routine. Without fail, she used the Regents Canal

THIRTY-FIVE

towpath to get to and from her apartment. To Harry, this was the stuff of which dreams were made. Anyone who sticks to a routine becomes an easy target. Random routes are the enemy of planned attacks. Now Harry had a plan, and tonight would be the night. Whether she entered the canal higher up or at Salmon Street lock, had no effect on his plan. A section of towpath ran alongside the canal only a few hundred metres from her apartment, and bordered by a selection of bushes; a section she always used. Granted, they were not the thickest of bushes, but given the light amount of foot traffic along this section of the canal, especially at the time of night she regularly came home, he would be unlucky indeed to be disturbed, so he would take the chance and do it right here. Only on one occasion did she use the steps from the A13 to the towpath, and Harry hoped this would not be the case tonight; she would not pass the bushes.

This killing would be different, her death would be slow, but extremely painful, he wanted her to know she was dying and why. Because of the proximity to the towpath, watching the last glimmer of life fade from her eyes would not be possible. Her dying would be slow; too risky for him to stay and wallow in the pleasure of her demise. No, he would have to be satisfied with knowing she saw the demons and suffered, and as a result, many young girls would no longer do so.

Harry felt the surge of adrenalin as a long shadow danced along the towpath on the far side of Salmon Lane; someone was coming this way. The shadow vanished as it reached the darkness cast by the nineteenth-century bridge. A figure emerged. There was no mistaking the sway in her hips as she walked. When younger, he might have made a play for her, but the knowledge of who she was and how she treated others wiped all such thoughts from his head. Tonight his dark side had control and the adrenalin flowed in anticipation of taking control of her life.

HARRY

His field of vision narrowed, extraneous noises faded away as his whole being concentrated on the target, the hunter focused entirely on its prey. At times like these Harry was no longer human, he became pure animal, the killer instinct as strong as in any lion. He moved silently and she remained unaware of his presence. The garrotte tightened around her neck before her mind registered she was not alone. She went limp almost immediately. Consciousness is soon lost after interruption of the blood supply to the brain. Harry adored this part; the beginning of ultimate control over another being.

Harry scanned the bridge over the canal and along the towpath in each direction looking for passers-by. He could still walk away and disappear into the maze of streets adjoining the canal at this stage if someone disturbed him. No one in sight. He dragged the unconscious woman into the bushes, pausing long enough to retrieve the Jimmy Choo high heel pulled off by the dragging. The pressure on her neck kept her unconscious, but was not enough to kill her. He didn't want to do that, not just yet.

He released some of the tension on the garrotte and she soon regained some of her senses but not before he'd given her a little injection. He bent forward to whisper in her ear as she lay face down on the grass.

"Hello, Black Widow." The fragrance of her Amouage Fate perfume dallied in his nostrils and he savoured the feel of her black, silky hair over his hand.

He turned her over so she could get her first look at her attacker. Her first and last; of that fact she remained blissfully ignorant.

If any doubts remained about what he was doing, they were soon dispelled by the torrent of invective she delivered. Unaware of the seriousness of her predicament, she mistook Harry for a common mugger, threatening him with the direst of consequences if he didn't release her.

"Oh no, my lovely. You are going nowhere. Today is

THIRTY-FIVE

Judgement Day."

Harry smiled. He had a very apt bible passage for this one.

HARRY

CHAPTER THIRTY-SIX

"He's making fools of us Davy. He's running rings around us."

DS Barnes drove an unmarked car, taking his boss to Tower Hamlets' Mortuary; a place she visited all too often these past few months. The Bible Killer, as the press now dubbed him, had taken his fourth victim, or so it would appear. The same MO with the ligature and the carved bible passage, but even though many of the details of the murders were not released to the press, it was still feasible this could be a copycat killing.

As the Senior Investigating Officer, Helene usually attended the post-mortems to ensure the continuity of evidence, and find out first-hand what direction the investigation may be heading. On occasion she sent a senior officer from her team, something she preferred to avoid whenever possible.

Even she had doubts whether they would catch this one. He was smart. Apart from the odd fibre at the scenes, which may or may not be his, he left little physical evidence linking him to any of the murders. Until now; finally, they recovered something that may be traceable.

THIRTY-SIX

"I have to admit he's clever Ma'am. The trick with the silver...what was it again?"

"Nitrate."

"Yeah that's it, silver nitrate. A stroke of genius, turning a white supremacist black. Leslie would be turning in his grave if he knew. Did you say exposure to sunlight turned him black?"

"I didn't. Dr Melbourne did. Apparently it's used in photographic processing, at least the old fashioned processing, not the digital printing we have nowadays. Photographers who processed their own work were often identifiable by the black marks on their hands. The silver halides, that's what turns the skin black. Irreversible, but in a living person, the skin regenerates and eventually the skin will go back to its normal colour as the old skin is replaced. Not for him though, he went to his grave as a black man. Can't say as I'm sorry."

"Ma'am?"

"Oh, I'm sorry he went to his grave," she paused. "I think. Not sorry he was black when he did. I do love the irony of it."

"Yes, Ma'am, and choking on his own leaflets, another clever touch. Brings a whole new meaning to ramming your message down someone's throat."

"I rather suspect that's what he wanted to convey. This killer is clever. I don't think he's taunting us; I think he's not even considering us. He's going about what he sees as his business, and his alone. Something triggered him, if only we knew what."

Helene wondered if she should ask Davy how he felt about a killer cleaning up the streets. Did he have mixed feelings as she did?

"What do you think about what this guy his doing, ignoring the legal aspects, of course?"

DS Barnes didn't answer straight away while he

concentrated on getting the car out onto Mile End Road from Globe Road, made trickier by the almost immediate right turn into White Horse Lane.

White Horse Lane? When did this road last witness a white horse travelling on it, if ever?

Once clear of the traffic, the detective answered.

"I don't agree with the taking of anyone's life, Ma'am, but I must admit he does seem to be removing some of the less savoury characters from the parish. The problem is, he's finding them before we do. Doesn't make us look good does it?"

Helene said nothing. Davy had a point. The latest victim was someone they tried to bring to justice many a time, but she covered her tracks well; any evidence they gathered on her was circumstantial at best and the CPS wanted far more than that. This killer targeted his victims with almost military precision. Helene rewound that last thought. Military, my god, why did I not think of that before. That would account for why no one ever saw him, he had done this sort of thing before.

"Davy, when you go back I want you to go through the witness statements again. Find out how many people interviewed near the scenes had military training, particularly elite units. You'll need to access MOD records. I think our killer is from a military background. It fits. He knows how to kill, how to move without being seen, and how to disappear." She tilted her head to one side deep in thought.

"Will they tell us if they were Special Forces or not?"
"Hmm?...oh, No, probably not. Look for 'special duties' in their records."

DS Barnes gave her a sideways glance.

"It wouldn't be the first time I've arrest..." She stopped mid-sentence.

"That could be it, the trigger. I want a full list of known associates of Brian Hamilton since he started living on the

THIRTY-SIX

streets. Correlate that with the information you manage to obtain from the MOD. Let's see if he associated with anyone he served with. If I'm right about this, what we have is revenge killings not random murders. Whoever is doing this is getting back at the people responsible for Hamilton's death."

"But he's not is he, Ma'am? I mean, as far as we know none of these people were involved in that."

"I don't believe it matters to him if he finds the actual culprit. As long as he is hitting back at the same group of people he's fulfilling his desire for revenge."

Davy risked another glance at his boss.

"Where did you learn all this?"

Helene laughed. "CSI?"

Davy snorted.

"West Palm Beach. They are big into their criminal profiling on that side of the pond. I was lucky to work a case in which the FBI were involved. I milked their profiler for all he was worth."

She smiled to herself. There was more than one meaning to that statement.

It wasn't long before they reached the mortuary, a nondescript single storey red-brick building at the rear of the Coroner's Court. This was not Helene's favourite task, but it was a necessary part of the job.

As she got out of the car she turned back to DS Barnes.

"All this will be yours one day, Davy. Then you too can get to see the dead bodies being cut up."

"Thanks, Ma'am, I think."

Helene laughed as she shut the door.

CHAPTER THIRTY-SEVEN

Even using every one of his charms and skills, amassed and finely honed over the years, Nicky struggled to gather any information on the death of Brian Hamilton, other than from the official police statement. He would usually manage to gather a snippet here, or a titbit there; someone would overhear someone else, another might brag about their deeds, but this time the silence overwhelmed him. Not a word from Lenny either. He couldn't be sure if that was because Lenny hadn't bothered to do anything, or if Lenny had suffered the same success. He was sure Lenny would do something, his instinct told him that deep down he was an honourable man.

Over time, Nicky built up a formidable list of informants, contacts, friends and acquaintances, any of whom would tip him off about something long before the other reporters got wind of it. Unlike some of his calling, he didn't need to bribe people to give him this information; they gave it because he was a likeable fellow and he made time for the average man in the street.

The only thing concrete from the police statement was

THIRTY-SEVEN

they were seeking more than one person in connection with their enquiries, and Nicky wondered if the persons responsible came from outside the area. Perhaps after Hamilton died, they moved on. His gut told him otherwise; they were locals. Everything about the culprits pointed to them having local knowledge; the railway bridge over the canal where Hamilton died did not have easy access; the towpath being located on the opposite side of the canal. Only someone from the area would know how to get there. Of course, some crackhead may have stumbled across the sleeping man and tried to rob him, but Nicky didn't think so. From what little information the police released in the form of a press bulletin, the attack appeared to be more of a deliberate act, not a mugging gone wrong. In any case, who mugs a homeless person? What is there to steal? Moreover, the other attacks took places in areas away from CCTV, away from the public, and no one saw anyone suspicious entering or leaving the area. These people knew the lay of the land.

A pity no physical evidence had been recovered from the locations of the other attacks, but hindsight is a wonderful thing. Up to then the attacks were deemed more of a nuisance and not worthy of SOCO attendance; merely statements taken, reports filed, patrols increased where the homeless gathered, that being as much as the police thought they could justify, and probably rightly so.

Brian Hamilton's death may have been accidental, but if you set out to cause bodily harm to someone, it could be argued any resulting death is no accident at all. Clearly these people intended harm, but Nicky didn't think they meant to kill.

The same could not be said of the Bible Killer. He set out with the intent of killing someone, but again, no one saw anything; almost as if all these attacks had been carried out by ghosts. He wondered if the two were somehow linked. Hamilton came first and then the Bible Killer. It would be worth bearing in mind. He would seek out the Old Man and run it past him. He knew the homeless in Tower Hamlets better than anyone.

Nicky looked at the email on his desktop; how he hated computers. They had their uses, word processing being much easier than typing and correcting on a typewriter. He conceded that at least. Large chunks of text could be moved around to make the story more readable, but all this instant contact stuff? No, he didn't like that at all. In the old days when he went on a job, he was on his own, no emails, no text message, no telephone, just him and the story. His thoughts went back to the Highlands of Scotland, twenty-five years ago, risking his life to call the newsroom from a call box on some god-forsaken moor. Well, he believed he was risking his life; certain that bears and wolves still roamed in Scotland.

Nowadays you hardly had time to draft your opening line without the editor emailing or phoning to chase for the full story. Today, no difference; the editor wanted to know what progress he'd made on the Bible Killer. He thought that was what Nicky was working on, and in part he was right, but another project sat on Nicky's computer. His article about the attacks on the homeless ran some weeks earlier and he wanted to write a more in-depth story about the plight of the homeless; how someone who had served Queen and Country lost his life this way. Whether he would persuade the editor to agree to run the story would be another matter; it was old news. So unless the editor saw some mileage in a sympathy article it wouldn't be published. The bottom line was all that mattered these days. It always had been to some extent, but the golden days of investigative journalism and in-depth articles seemed to be over. Unless a radical changed occurred, not only in what the people wanted to read about, but also what the papers would do to obtain a story, then a rocky

THIRTY-SEVEN

road to ruin lay in the future of news journalism. In any event, he could always offer his piece to one of the weeklies under one of his pseudonyms.

Nicky wondered why the editor couldn't get off his arse, some twenty feet away, and come and ask in person. With the touch of a malevolent smile on his lips, Nicky marked the email as spam and watched it vanish from his inbox. Computers did have their uses after all. If only someone could do that in real life

.

CHAPTER THIRTY-EIGHT

'By-line by Nick Rolands.' Those words stuck in Donald Munro's craw. The pages of the paper fluttered to the grease stained carpet of the tiny apartment as Munro flung it across the room in his rage. How dare that punk of a kid continue his normal life after getting him locked up for twenty-five years? Munro still thought of him as a kid, even though Rolands was now middle aged. Life stood still for Munro when he went inside. Only now had the clock started to tick again. The clock certainly ticked for Rolands, counting down his last moments on this planet.

Munro stared out of the dirty window, framed by curtains that probably saw the Queen's coronation, and perhaps even VE day. What a shithole of a place he lived in now. When he thought back to his life before going inside; the luxuries, the comfort, the beautiful art, and now this; a stinking bedsit that should have been condemned long ago. Advertised as a compact studio apartment by the estate agent, Munro had no other option but take it; his choice of housing somewhat limited by his status of being 'out on licence.'

After all these years he felt no longer able to rely on

THIRTY-EIGHT

street informants for information, and struggled to find a way to reach Rolands. He could, of course, try to follow him from his offices, but he thought that might be too risky. After all, newspaper reporters were supposed to be alert to unusual activity; part of the job description. In any case the explosion in the number of CCTV cameras in the City over the last twenty-five years made it all but impossible to be in a public place unseen. Orwell would be shouting, 'I told you so,' from the highest hilltop if he'd still been alive. Munro couldn't risk being spotted on CCTV footage once Rolands met his fate, so he needed some way of getting to him unseen. Now this article by Rolands gave Munro something to work with.

Finally, he had the answer, and Rolands had given it to him on a plate. He might not be able to look for him at his place of employment, but now he knew exactly where to go and who to watch. He would rue the day he testified against him and Munro would savour every moment of the demise of Nicky Rolands.

CHAPTER THIRTY-NINE

A mortuary examination table is a great leveller. Rich, poor, black or white; when laid out on that table everyone is the same. What made this body stand out more than most was the hypodermic needle stuck in one eye. Not something you see every day, nor something you would want to, if it came to that.

"Do we know who she is?"

Helene answered. "Phuong Nguyen, aka 'Miss Fi', known to us but we never managed to catch her doing anything illegal; a proper slippery customer. Suspected drug dealer and reputed to run a string of girls. Vicious bitch from all accounts, gets them hooked on the drugs, puts them on the game, then when they lose their earning capacity, cuts them off and boots them out. You saw the photographs from the site?"

One of James Melbourne's colleagues attended the murder scene, but the post-mortem fell to James.

"Yes. Certainly seems to be the same partial MO so are we thinking this may be the same perpetrator? What was the bible passage this time?"

THIRTY-NINE

James pointed the figures M6:13 carved into the woman's left thigh. She had been positioned with her skirt pulled up, her pants removed, and her legs apart at the knees with the feet placed together.

"And lead us not into temptation, but deliver us from the evil one. Kind of appropriate for her, I would say."

James nodded. "They've all been appropriate. Whoever is doing this knows his Bible it seems."

"And his victims, apparently. Hardly the work of a god fearing man though is it?"

"Oh I don't know. All that eye for an eye and tooth for a tooth stuff in the Old Testament. For some, the interpretation might mean exactly this. He's only targeted known criminals so far hasn't he?"

Helene shook her head. "As obnoxious as Leslie might have been, he operated within the law, but as far as we are aware, the murderer hasn't killed at random, although we can't be a hundred percent sure there aren't any others and we've not found them yet, as for being known criminals, he latched onto the rapist before we did. In some ways I wish I had him on my team."

James raised an eyebrow.

"Oh you know what I mean, James. He's hitting the underbelly of the criminal world, maybe not the organised stuff, but he's certainly removing some of the pond life."

If anything, James' eyebrow went even further, partially joined by its sibling.

"It sounds as if you admire him, Helene."

Helene cocked her head to one side.

"No. Admire, isn't the right word, understand him maybe, but not admire. You can see where I'm coming from though can't you?"

The eyebrows assumed their natural position on James' forehead.

"I understand the frustration you must feel when the CPS decide not to prosecute for 'lack of evidence'." He delivered the last three words in a mimicking voice.

"You don't know the half of it, James. Some of these characters are completely Teflon coated and literally get away with murder. Not the ones this guy is after. They're the minor league. I'm talking about the organised stuff. They think... no, they are sure they're untouchable. We don't get as much as a sniff on them, but we know who the players are, and what's worse, they know we know and they laugh at us. Then, if by some miracle we put one in a cell, in pops their brief and within an hour they're walking. I'd love to have a shot at those people. This guy is working outside the law and achieving what we can't when we work within it. Just who does the law protect? Makes you think, doesn't it?"

James looked her in the eyes. She could see he wasn't convinced about what she said, and she knew her job was to uphold the law, but sometimes, just once in a while, the law is truly an ass.

"Shall we start?" he asked, finally.

Helene nodded. She wasn't particularly squeamish but neither was she keen on the sight of the hypodermic protruding from the woman's eye. She witnessed far worse things in her work, but something about that gave her the shivers. Even from an early age, Helene had a fear of anything near her eyes; she couldn't wear contact lenses. Even the sight of someone putting one in, or taking it out, made her turn away, and this from the woman who saw more mutilated bodies than most.

"Let me know when you are going to take that out," with her face screwed up she nodded towards the hypodermic. "You don't want to be picking me up off the floor, and you will be doing if you don't warn me first."

She didn't enjoy this part of the job at all. As she moved up the ranks, only rarely did she get tasked to

THIRTY-NINE

attend a post-mortem, but once she became the senior officer, it became part of her job description. This time she felt it to be more important than ever; this possibly being the fourth victim of what now appeared to be a serial killer.

The previous three victims exhibited the same partial MO; ligature marks to the neck, not the cause of death, and a link to a bible passage carved somewhere in the victims' skin. The actual cause of death had been different in each case, but appropriate to the circumstances of the victim.

She would lay odds on the COD for this one being a drug overdose, more than likely delivered through the hypodermic that James would soon be removing from the eye. She didn't disturb him when he worked; she observed. As to be expected from someone with his reputation and standing within the forensic science community, his approach, as ever, methodical and thorough; often he spotted something minuscule that on more than one occasion 'cracked the case wide open' as the cliché would put it. They made an excellent team, and that is what this job was all about, teamwork.

Briefly she wondered if they would make a great team in their personal lives, then dismissed the thought as quickly as it arrived. That would not happen. James had a wife and she would not be responsible for a break up. Not when there were so many willing single men available. She brought her mind back to the present. How could she be having those thoughts when someone a body lay on a slab in front of her? Had she really become so detached from it all? She didn't think so, if anything, as she got older she became more personally involved in some of the cases. Perhaps it was only these victims she had doubts about, the dregs, the trouble makers. She knew they didn't deserve to die, especially not the way they did, but part of her felt they were getting some just deserts. She would certainly lose no sleep over it.

As James started to wrap up his examination, he turned to Helene.

"Nothing I can see to indicate any trauma that would be COD so I'm expecting the tox reports will show some sort of narcotic. Damage to the lungs was pretty evident, and the pink froth is a good indicator of an opiate overdose. She had no signs of being a user, so whoever is doing this must have known this would be a particularly nasty way for her to go, especially in the eye like that."

"How on earth did he manage to do that without her fighting? Her eyes are open."

"That's a good point Helene. I'll get a screen for neuromuscular blockers. They don't always show but we can give it a go. Given where he was I doubt something like Rohypnol would be quick enough. He would need something fast acting, as used in theatre. More than likely she would still be able to feel pain, but with the muscles relaxed, she wouldn't be able to react to it. Unless he gave her a sufficient dose to stop her breathing, she would have suffered immensely. You know, we may be looking at a medical professional for this. He seems to know what he is doing."

Helene smiled under her surgical mask; she couldn't resist the temptation.

"So, Doctor, where were you this morning between the hours of one and four?"

James took a step back and stammered "I... I..."

Helene dissolved in a fit of giggles.

CHAPTER FORTY

The telephone on DS Barnes' desk rang, interrupting the morning briefing. DCI MacKay motioned for him to answer, and waited for him to finish. She cocked her head to one side in question.

"You're not going to like this, Ma'am."

"If it's another body, Davy, you're not wrong."

Barnes shook his head, "Not quite, Ma'am, but almost as bad. The attacks on the homeless have started again. Two last night. A couple of broken ribs and swollen eyes. Both will be okay after a couple of days of rest according to the doctors."

Helene swore under her breath, then turned to DI Renton.

"Adam, I'm going to ask you to run with this and to continue with the murder investigation for Hamilton, as they are linked. I'll head up the investigation for our serial killer." She shook her head. "All we need now is for him to dish up another body for us, and our lives will be complete."

She glanced around the room. "Take Mary and Mike, but I can't spare any more. I'll speak to Uniform about assigning a couple more bodies to assist. You may as well stay for the briefing on the serial case. Heaven knows how much might be relevant to you. In fact, we'll continue with joint briefings. Something tells me all of these cases are linked somehow. Right, where were we?"

The briefing continued, bringing everyone up to date with the cases so far. Four victims of the serial killer, all with ligature marks and all tortured in some way before they died. The killer enjoyed what he did. Although strictly speaking they kept an open mind on the gender of the killer, they always referred to the perpetrator as he; statistically a serial killer was far more likely to be male, and in the case of Worthing, highly unlikely a woman would be strong enough to overpower him, or to kill him in that way.

Matching DNA evidence, in the form of hairs, had been recovered from two of the scenes, but with nothing on the database to match them against, there was no mileage in that. Forensically there appeared to be little else to go on. The killer appeared to be aware of forensic techniques, and left very little of himself at any of the scenes. No one saw or heard anything unusual, and in three of the cases, although he left the bodies concealed, the nature of the concealment meant the killer not only expected, but almost certainly wanted them to be discovered eventually. The carving of Bible references on the bodies helped to reinforce this idea. He wanted everyone to know why these people died. So far the details of the bible references had not been released to the press. The less the public knew, the less likelihood of copycat killings.

As anticipated, the MOD were less than forthcoming about service records, and the enquiries slowed down by the fact that anyone who had already made a statement needed to be re-interviewed regarding any military service. This took time, but as in all detective work, the methodical gathering of information would eventually lead to the killer. Solving crimes was more akin to a marathon than a sprint.

"On the subject of the killer being ex-military, I'm aware of the slow progress at the MOD, and some of the persons who gave statements are proving difficult to contact," Helene shrugged. "There's a contact who might be able to shed some light on ex-military personnel on the streets. Quite a few of the rough sleepers are ex-forces. I'll see if he can come up with any ideas about the attacks."

"If you'll forgive me for saying, Ma'am, most of the ones I've seen couldn't kick back at a paper bag, let alone some of the victims."

"You might be right, Danny, but we have nothing else so far, and one or two are still fit enough, certainly enough to do this anyway. So, unless someone walks in to ask us to test his DNA, and I think there is more chance of Millwall winning the Champion's League, we'll keep chipping away until we come up with something concrete."

"Excuse me, Ma'am. We're on a roll, you know," exclaimed DC Holland.

"So were Bonnie and Clyde, Johnny, and look where it got them."

A ripple of laughter spread around the room, lightening the sombre mood.

Helene studied the whiteboard containing the key points of their information.

"What are we missing here? Other than they are all known to us. What else might they have in common? Different backgrounds, different areas, time of death for three of the four is the early hours, but the fourth, late evening. Three male, one female, so it isn't a gender thing. Even the COD, two choking, one beating and one OD. The only commonality is the ligature marks and the bible passages."

DS Barnes echoed what he suggested in the car. "Maybe that's it, Ma'am. They are all known to us, that is the common denominator. Maybe that is what the killer is doing, helping us clear up, in his own sweet way."

FORTY

Helene nodded. "You may be right. I'd love to be able to ask him, but first we need to nick him. Anything else from anyone?"

With nothing new raised, Helene brought the briefing to a close. "Go find me a killer."

They were not much closer now than at the start, and three more bodies lay in the mortuary. She would see what her contact could come up with. She didn't hold out much hope.

ooOoo

The Old Man listened without interruption as the detective made her request.

"There are a few of us who are ex-military, and probably one or two special forces. I don't mean the ones who talk about it all the time and say they are, those are the wannabes, the ones who never served in a special unit. Whether any of them will open up I'm not sure. Most of the special forces guys don't want to talk about their experiences."

He put his head in his hands and sighed, then looked at her, his eyes glistening with the first sign of tears.

"He didn't deserve that, no one does. You think one of our own killed Brian?"

Helene reached out for his hand and held it between hers. She noticed he referred to ex-military as 'our own.' She knew little about the Old Man, other than he was streetwise. They never talked about his background, only the present. If he wanted to tell her, he would do, otherwise it remained none of her business.

She came across him by chance a few years previous whilst on an enquiry into a robbery. He saw it happen and he proved to be an observant witness. Since then, she kept in touch with him, bringing him food and drink on a regular basis. A pleasant soul to talk to once he opened up to you. Cantankerous at times, of course, but then who wasn't? Of what little she did know about him, the fact St Mary's appeared to be his favourite haunt was at the top of the list. Always the first place she came to when she wanted to find him.

"No. But I think an ex-soldier might be responsible for the other murders."

They sat in silence for several minutes, each in their own thoughts.

Eventually the Old Man spoke.

"You're not looking for Brian's killer?"

"I'm not, but my team still are, and they are very good. I know, I picked them. We will find the ones responsible for Brian. I promise."

Helene did not often make those promises. Sometimes they could not be fulfilled, so she avoided them. On this occasion, she vowed she would do her utmost to ensure she delivered.

"Just do the best you can to get someone to talk, that's all I can ask. I don't mind telling you we're struggling. We've nothing to go on, well, nothing significant. Not only for these murders but for Brian's too. It's as if we're dealing with ghosts."

The Old Man agreed to do his best, and Helene left him in the churchyard soaking up the remains of the afternoon sun, with a single tear running down his cheek.

CHAPTER FORTY-ONE

A few weeks had passed since Nicky visited Lenny to ask for his assistance. In that time the attacks on the homeless stopped and he wondered if that was anything to do with Lenny, or merely a coincidence. At roughly the same time, the violent rapes witnessed in the area also come to an abrupt and messy end when the rapist turned up mutilated and murdered. Rough Justice, but well deserved, Nicky thought. He speculated who would do that, perhaps one of the rapist's potential victims, or one he had already attacked, perhaps even the partner of one. It seemed too brutal a crime for a woman to commit, considering the way the man died, choking on his own doodad; the thought made Nicky mentally cross his legs, as would most men. He could see that being the work of a woman wronged, although it would take one tough lady to do that in the midst of an assault.

With no fresh attacks on the homeless, the editor reassigned Nicky to other stories, but when spare moments arose he still worked on the Hamilton case and

FORTY-ONE

the attacks leading up to it, and sometimes he would continue working on it when he should be concentrating on something else. He decided to postpone his resignation plans and see this story through with the full resources of a major newspaper. Access to databases throughout the world remained a far easier prospect from within the news offices. Some were available through a local library, but finding a library was getting more and more difficult; many branches falling victim to council cutbacks. Nicky wondered if maybe keeping the populace ignorant so they couldn't challenge the government of the day was part of the plan.

Once Nicky found some answers about Brian, he would take stock of his situation. Doing things on impulse almost cost him his life twenty-five years ago. Now he thought things through a bit more thoroughly before committing himself to a course of action.

Another routine day passed at the office and Nicky was happy to be on his way home, on time for once. This evening he would ignore work, chill out, listen to some music, down a couple of glasses of wine and curl up with a favourite book. He looked forward to his 'me' time. His only other 'me' time, his monthly massage. He and the masseuse would put the world to rights before he drifted away as he relaxed. His masseuse knew exactly when to stop talking.

As he pushed the key into the lock, the door clicked and swung open. Strange, he always locked it, without fail, and he was certain he locked it this morning. Someone must have been in his flat. No sign of a forced entry, just the door not quite latched. The first prickle of apprehension made him shiver; what if an intruder was still inside? He didn't know whether to enter or not. All those years of caution, and not doing things on impulse went out of the window as finally his curiosity got the better of him. He took care stepping inside so as not to make a sound. He couldn't hear anyone, but even so, he waited a full minute before venturing further. He picked up his Fox umbrella from the corner in the hall, not quite as useful as a shotgun, but as he didn't possess one of those, the umbrella would suffice. He quietly worked his way from the hall to the living room. With the umbrella raised as a modern day sword, he poked his head around the door and carefully surveyed the room. Nothing appeared to be out of place, as far as he could tell. That didn't mean there hadn't been an intruder, but the motive clearly not theft. The more he looked, the more he became convinced no one had been there, not one solitary item appeared out of place. Nicky checked each room in turn, found them to be the same, and calmed down. Obviously he didn't lock the door this morning when he left. In his mind he felt certain he did, but his mind fooled him before. Confusing one event with a similar or identical one was a well-known phenomenon. The less remarkable and more repetitious, the easier it became to confuse the brain as a sequence of similar events began to emerge into one. That must be it. He forgot: nothing more. Plenty occupied his mind at the moment.

A nice bit of Mozart, that would calm him. He selected Violin Concerto No 3 from his vast collection of both classical and contemporary music. Mozart made him relax. How could anyone stay tense with the sweet pure notes of a violin floating around? He turned on the reading lamp by his chair and set the rest of the room lighting to low. With an Australian Merlot in his hand he settled down to continue reading the second in Asimov's Foundation series, Foundation and Empire. The second in the original trilogy; altogether, Asimov wrote a total of seven in the series, including two prequels. Nicky loved sci-fi, and in particular Asimov. He'd read them all before, but he wanted a good, well-constructed story. It would take him away from the troubles of the real world for a while.

Nicky glanced at the clock on the wall. That's when

the memories of that night twenty-five years ago came flooding back to him, the cold tendrils of fear touching his soul as real now as then. His mouth went dry and his neck rigid. He dropped the glass, which shattered on the parquet floor, scattering shards of glass. Lenny's warning came flooding back to him. How did he not see that before? Someone had been in his flat; someone who knew exactly which buttons to press. The one person who he hoped would leave him alone after all this time; a hope that just shattered like the glass now lying in an ever widening stain of red liquid on the floor. Donald Munro had been the intruder and he left a calling card, one that let Nicky know he could reach him anytime, anywhere.

Sitting on the top of the clock, a single link from a length of anchor chain.

CHAPTER FORTY-TWO

John Harrison was dead. His body and mind not aware of it yet, but the moment he broke into the church his death became inevitable. Some would say it was the hand of God, many would say it was deserved, few would mourn his passing.

Had he chosen a different path he may have lived, but fate brought him to this place, at this precise moment and John Harrison ceased to be.

He didn't give a damn though, he needed more drugs, and for drugs he needed money. They had collections in churches, so where there were churches there would be money, and money provided a means to buy drugs. All this made sense in Harrison's mind. That the money might be moved elsewhere after the service never occurred to him. Nor did it cross his mind that Sunday would be a better day of the week to break in. No - the only thing in his head, the equation church equals money, money equals drugs. Perhaps with a little more guidance, he may have been on a different path. Life is full of possibilities and choices and at some time or other we all make the wrong one. For Harrison, the wrong one would be his last.

FORTY-TWO

He didn't often go inside a church; the last time being when his gran died. He found them to be spooky, big, hollow buildings with still air and creepy pictures in the windows and on the walls. The silence inside the church lay at odds with its proximity to the road, but that seemed to be the case with all churches, as if extraneous noise was forbidden to enter. As for creepy pictures, this place sported the creepiest paintings he had ever seen. Not that he saw many in his life. Not his cup of tea at all. A pint down the pub, the match at a weekend, and the rest of the time high on a line of coke, or whatever he laid his hands on. A man of simple tastes.

Luck smiled on him tonight. The building was undergoing some sort of renovation work. A good chance of power tools on the premises; much better than cash from the collection. They always made a few quid down the pub. He would move them on before anyone noticed them missing; almost as good as cash itself.

Getting in proved to be easy; the back door no match for his crowbar and he soon jemmied it open. No alarm system either. You would think they would know by now to fit alarms; alarms are a pain in the arse.

He rummaged around and soon found the power tools. He rooted through them to find the most expensive looking ones. He couldn't take them all.

He thought he heard a sound at the door and froze. John learned the art of keeping silent from being in other people's bedrooms; the ones he entered without permission. Occasionally, they would move in their sleep and he would take on all the aspects of a statue.

After several minutes of focusing his hearing to detect the slightest noise, he decided it was his imagination, and went back to his search.

The pain across his throat came so suddenly and intensely, he didn't have time to react. Briefly aware of something moving, then agony. He felt himself being dragged backwards by whatever sliced into his neck. His vision closed in; an ever decreasing tunnel of darkness, until finally, nothing.

ooOoo

What would a young lad like that be doing sneaking into the grounds of the church at this time of night? Harry thought it unlikely he would be going to pray; especially with what looked like a jemmy sticking out of the bottom of his jacket. The lad looked around nervously; not the actions of someone with a legitimate reason to be there. After a furtive glance around, he entered the shadows at the rear of the church, and shortly after, Harry heard the unmistakable sound of splintering wood. How dare he enter the House of God in such a way? Had he no respect at all? Like those in the churchyard where he caught the rapist, he undoubtedly respected no one, not even himself.

Maybe he forgot his key, thought Harry, smiling, knowing full well this young man would soon be in his clutches. After giving him a few moments to get inside, Harry slipped through the broken door, avoiding the splinters of wood poking out from the jamb, where the jemmy made short work of the lock. Harry crouched as he entered the vestibule to avoid being silhouetted in the doorway, then paused to allow his eyes to become accustomed to the darkness. It would be lighter inside the body of the church as light spilled through the windows from the street lamps outside, but in the back, the only light came from the door he just entered.

Now inside, the young man clearly no longer felt the need to be quiet, and Harry could hear him rummaging around somewhere; probably through the tools left overnight by the builders carrying out the renovations. Did he not know how bad it was to steal from the House of God? Well, he would soon find out and be taught a lesson; one that he would remember for the remainder of his short life.

FORTY-TWO

Harry checked his pocket again; his friend still there, he expected nothing less, his friend being the only constant in his life; the only thing he could rely on. And now they worked as a team again, they were unstoppable. He could see the young man now, not much more than a boy. Tough luck, he shouldn't commit such a sin. The lad's attention lay focused solely on the power tools at his feet. Harry moved quietly, knowing his next victim would not be aware of his presence until too late.

He pulled the wire tight around his victim's neck and stepped backwards. The young man grabbed for his throat then almost immediately became limp. Harry would need to drag this wretch of a human closer to the altar, his mind working on an idea of where to lay him. Once he managed to pull him into the chancel he thought of a much better idea.

Aware the young man would be unconscious for a few minutes, Harry returned to the corner of the transept where the power tools lay scattered. He soon found what he wanted and made his way back to the chancel as the young man started to come round. Harry applied the pressure once again to the youth's neck and he slipped back into unconsciousness. With the lad in place beneath the cross he allowed him to come round again; he would need his co-operation: for a short while at least.

The boy shook his head, still groggy from being unconscious, and still unaware of Harry's presence.

"Strip to your underwear."

The voice startled him, but then he became defiant as he studied Harry's face.

"Fuck off, you old pervert. Find your kicks elsewhere."

The tip of Harry's knife penetrated the skin under the young man's chin.

"I said, strip."

No argument this time, only fear in his eyes.

Once down to his underwear, Harry made him stand with his back against the wall. His defiance returned, but the short, sharp pain he received as the rigid fingers jabbed into his stomach persuaded him to do as he was told. He was still a little unsteady and when ordered to spread his arms wide, like a tree, he complied with a look of puzzlement on his face.

"I hope you aren't thinking of giving me a blow-job, cos if you are..."

He never got to finish his sentence as the first nail penetrated his right hand, pinning it to the wall. Anticipating his movement, Harry slammed the lad's left arm back and repeated his action to the left hand. A nail gun has many uses, but Harry would wager crucifixion would not be on the manufacturer's list.

"Jesus Christ..." The words came out as a more of a squeal than spoken.

"If you would take the time to look up, you will find he is watching over you."

Harry smiled.

"Now I have your undivided attention, you and I are going to have a little talk. You see, I think that in your youth...Oh listen to me, your youth. What am I saying? You are still a youth. Okay, I think in the early part of your childhood, mummy and daddy, you did have a daddy didn't you?" Harry didn't wait for an answer. "Mummy and daddy neglected to take you to church, because if they had, you would know how wrong it is to steal. Now what makes it worse is you are stealing from the House of God."

The lad sobbed.

"I wasn't going to nick anything from the church, just from the builders, honest, mister. Please let me go."

Harry continued as if he hadn't heard a word. Nothing better than having a captive audience to deliver a message to; this particular audience being far more captive than most.

CHAPTER FORTY-THREE

As churches go, St John on Bethnal Green couldn't be called the prettiest in London, with its mix of stone pillars and red brick walls, but by no means was it the ugliest either. Once inside, the arch braced truss roof made it look older than its hundred and fifty years. Galleries ran full length over the aisles on either side of the nave and brought a light and airy touch to the interior.

That contrasted with Helene's feeling of darkness with the discovery of the fifth murder, in only three months. The fifth from the Bible Killer anyway. They were no closer with solving Brian Hamilton's murder either.

"Oh Jesus," Helene said.

"You aren't the first to say that, and I can see what would make you think so, but I'm afraid you're wrong. He's a few feet further up."

The black humour that sometimes crept into the job probably kept them all sane.

DCI MacKay and Dr Melbourne studied the body of a young man nailed to the wall behind the pulpit steps, a parody of the crucifix above. Beneath, a sticky reddish-brown river created a macabre waterfall, having dripped

FORTY-THREE

off the dado to form a lake of life lost on the tiled floor of the north transept.

She studied the rest of the church. The paintings on display did nothing to improve her mood: the fourteen stations of the cross. Her childhood church boasted beautiful stained glass windows depicting the same scenes, and as a catholic, the meaning of each were ingrained into her soul. These paintings had been commissioned by the church and were a relatively recent addition, but this was the first time she had seen them in all their glory. They had an air of gloom about them, something that seemed to scream inside her head, but then the subject was no laughing matter.

"Poor bugger. Do we have an identity?"

"John Harrison, apparently. Sergeant Gupta has the details. He recognised him straight away. Who says bobbies on the streets aren't needed eh?" He paused. "The blood on the palms around the nails, along with that on the floor, would indicate he was nailed while still alive. I'm not sure if he would be conscious, but I'm guessing he would be. Based on the amount of blood, at this stage I'm guessing COD to be exsanguination, I would imagine caused by the wounds on both wrists. As usual, I'll be able to determine more after the post-mortem. The usual ligature marks are present, and as you can see..."

The doctor pointed to the bloody figures on his chest.

Helene swore strongly.

"Sorry, Doc. Too many of these. My nerves are getting a little bit frazzled. I'll put Barnes on to translating that."

"You and me both. Getting too many early morning calls to suspicious deaths for my liking."

Helene sighed. "I can't remember the last long lie in. How long before we can take him down?"

"Another three or four hours at least. Not the easiest place to work."

"I suppose not, well..."

"Let you know when I have something, Helene?"

"I think we have worked together for too long, Doc."

"Haven't we just."

Sergeant Gupta finished taking a statement from the unfortunate cleaner who discovered the body. Helene waited until a WPC led away the shaken cleaner, pulled the hood from her head and shook her hair loose.

"Okay, fill me in, Sergeant."

"Ma'am. John Harrison, nineteen years of age, local scally. String of convictions for burglaries, petty theft and drugs. From the looks of it he intended to nick something from here. Found a door forced at the back, and a crowbar inside. Bit dodgy being so close to the road. Could easily be spotted. Power tools scattered around over there."

"I think it's safe to say someone did spot him, unless someone was already in here."

"Not sure what he thought he would find in a church these days unless he already knew about the tools in here."

"He found God, I think." Helene glanced back towards the pulpit. "They don't really care do they? They'll nick anything to pay for a fix. What about the cleaner?"

"Mrs Evans. Been cleaning here for twenty-three years. Came in at six this morning, discovered the body around six twenty-five. Triple nine call timed at six thirty-two. Called in by a passer-by. Apparently Mrs Evans believes a telephone should be tied to the wall. Doesn't believe in these new-fangled mobiles."

Helene frowned.

"Is there not a phone on the premises?"

The Sergeant shook his head.

"Apparently not."

"You said it was some twenty-five minutes before she discovered the body."

"She says she didn't notice it straight away because of

the pulpit, she only saw him when she came around this side and noticed the blood."

Helene smiled.

"Thanks, Sergeant." She closed her eyes for a moment, the index finger of her left hand on her nose, and her thumb under her chin.

"Okay, I'm going to second you to my team for a while. I'm shorthanded. I'll clear it with the inspector. I want you to see what you can find out about known associates, from neighbours, family etc. I don't think we'll have much luck there, but you never know. What particularly interests me is whether he was alone or with an accomplice."

"You don't think this is linked to the others then, Ma'am?"

"More than likely, Sergeant, but we must consider all possibilities."

HARRY

CHAPTER FORTY-FOUR

The Old Man sat on the Stairway to Heaven War memorial in Bethnal Green Gardens. He moved his jaws making random chewing motions as many old people did. Across the street the Church of St John On Bethnal Green had become the centre of some intense police activity, and although it appeared to be concentrated inside, there was still plenty to be seen going on in the grounds. On occasion, white suited figures appeared, like earthly analogies of spectral parishioners.

It didn't take a genius to work out someone had died here, and judging from the activity, they were treating the death as suspicious. The SOCO van parked in the church driveway bore testament to that, and the fact that Roman Road remained cordoned off during rush hour. I bet that's causing chaos, the Old Man thought; glad he didn't drive, well not anymore.

One of the white suited figures emerged and motioned to a man in normal clothing on the edge of the tape barrier. They engaged in conversation for a few moments then he moved away to a police minibus parked behind the SOCO van. Another conversation ensued, and soon a line of uniformed officers spewed from the bus like ants from a nest; less in number, only twelve of them, but they seemed to number far more. They gathered around the queen ant, in this case merely a sergeant, before scattering in several directions, one of those being the park.

The Old Man knew what was happening, door-to-door enquiries, and as he didn't have a door he would come under 'and anyone in the vicinity' enquiries.

"Good morning, Sir," said the uniformed twelve-year-old.

At least that's how old he appeared to be to the Old Man, who acknowledged him with a grunt. He had nothing against coppers unless being moved on from a comfy sleeping place.

"Can you tell me how long you've been here?"

The Old Man, continued chewing his mouthful of nothing before uttering, "Nope."

The officer's head moved back sharply. Not the answer he expected.

"That's not very co-operative, Sir."

The Old Man chewed a while more before answering.

"Maybe not, but it's the truth," and pointed to his wrist. "I don't have a watch, Sonny. I can't answer your question."

The officer sighed and rethought his question, finally eliciting that the Old Man arrived sometime after the Police, but before they cordoned off the road, and had been there ever since. No, he didn't see or hear anything suspicious but he wouldn't mind the price of a cup of tea if the officer could spare some change. Sighing heavily again he handed over a £2 coin.

When the policeman asked for the Old Man's name, he seemed reluctant to accept that everyone called him the Old Man, but finally he conceded the point and wrote it down in his notebook.

HARRY

The Old Man stopped his chewing and searched the young constable's face for clues. He could swear he had just been asked for his address.

"Are you being serious, Sonny?" The Old Man studied him again. "Did they not teach you anything at that school of yours?"

The officer seemed puzzled. "School?"

"Aye, well, I was referring to the police college or whatever it is they call it nowadays. But come to think of it I might as well be talking about your primary school too. You seem to have a lack of understanding of the word 'homeless'. You did go to school didn't you?"

The policeman smiled.

"I need a contact address in case of further questions."

"You are serious aren't you? The Streets of London, and I don't mean with Ralph McTell."

The officer look puzzled. "I need a bit more than that, Sir."

"In that case, Sonny, go and ask Prime-Minister Fancy-Pants to do something about the homeless of this fair land. Though I suspect he is more concerned about his trust funds and offshore investments. But until he addresses the issue, 'London' will suffice as my address. If you like I can narrow it down to 'the East End,' but that's all you're getting."

With that the Old Man got up and shuffled away through the gardens leaving behind a rapidly reddening police officer, pencil poised over his notebook and still waiting for an answer to the question of the Old Man's address.

ooOoo

Hastily dropping his cigarette and grinding it into the ground, a lone figure set off in pursuit of the old man. So far his surveillance had not paid off, but it would soon; he was sure of that. Had he taken the time to glance behind him, his certainty may have taken something of a knock.

The first rule of surveillance; make sure you don't have your own tail. In his dim and distant past, he would have been aware of his watcher, but so intent was he on his own prey, it never crossed his mind he too could be followed.

With his feet hardly ever leaving the ground, the old boy didn't so much walk as roller skate, without the rollers, sliding his tatty shoes along the floor. He kept up a surprising pace in this fashion, and the tail wondered how he managed to do that in such a decrepit pair of shoes. A passing thought and one of little importance. What mattered was where this old geezer might lead him.

Away from the tube station entrance, the park appeared less busy than he hoped. It proved hard to blend in with the crowd, when there wasn't one. Fortunately, the old man never looked back

All his hopes were pinned on this old codger leading him to where he so desperately wanted to be, he prayed he wouldn't let him down.

CHAPTER FORTY-FIVE

"Not quite what I had in mind."

James struggled to make himself heard over the noise in the pub as two men tried to knock each other to the floor with the crowd cheering them on; the fight being a live boxing match on a large screen TV in the corner and which held the attention of the majority of the clientele.

"What kind of cheapskate do you think I am, James?"
"One that buys a packet of crisps and calls it a meal?"

Helene cocked her head on one side. "If I thought for one minute you were serious..."

"If I thought for one minute, you thought I was being serious, I would've said it from over by the door, ready for a quick getaway."

The Salmon and Ball Public House was on the opposite corner of the junction to St John's Church. Once things were wrapped up at the scene, Helene suggested they go for a drink to wind down. James, for once agreed.

As these things are in a habit of doing, the quiet drink turned into something of a prolonged session. The pair needed to let off steam, and alcohol provided the quickest way of doing so.

"Shouldn't you be getting home, James?"

"No rush. Beth's gone to see her folks in Chippenham. Cold, dark house is all that's waiting for me." He muttered into his pint. "Cold most of the time, these days."

Helene frowned. "Sorry James I..."

He held up his hand and shook his head. "Nothing important."

"In that case, your round."

James' eyebrow did its journey north again." It's always my round."

"That's because pathologists are paid more than DCI's. Speaking of getting home, how are you doing that? You're not driving, 'cos I'd be forced to nick you."

"I don't have the car. I told my assistant to take it back to the mortuary."

She smiled. "Good thinking, Batman."

"What about you?"

"Same way as you I suppose, taxi."

Like many who are slightly over the odds with their drink, they fell into silence, staring into their glasses.

Helene spoke first.

"What I don't understand, James, is how the killer got him to stand there while he nailed the poor bugger to the wall? He wasn't a tiny lad, was he?"

"My guess is he's skilled with the ligature. He can keep people at an altered state of consciousness." James stopped for a moment." Although there's been nothing to suggest more than one assailant, there could be, you know."

"Don't you dare suggest we've more than one crazed killer on the loose, James Melbourne. I've enough on my plate with this one. Not to mention we still haven't got a lead on Hamilton's killers."

HARRY

A cheer went up from in front of the big screen TV. The referee stood over a figure lying on the canvas, his index finger counting the seconds to the end of the fighter's participation in this bout.

Helene got to her feet, unlike the boxer on the TV who still lay supine while the victor paraded around the ring, punching the air.

"Come on, let's get out of here. We'll grab a taxi and you can drop me on the way."

CHAPTER FORTY-SIX

After the elation of taking another life, Harry found himself sinking into another bout of depression. This was not an uncommon cycle in the life of a serial killer, which is why they went on to kill again and again. Only the high of another kill could remedy the self-loathing they felt afterwards; a vicious circle of delight and despair, only broken by being caught.

For Harry it was different. He didn't feel any remorse for their deaths, only sadness it had to be this way. Why could people not be nice to each other? We all lived on an insignificant rock orbiting a star on the edge of a galaxy. In the grand scheme of things, we didn't matter and yet we were hell-bent on screwing each other over. That's where the sadness came from. Just how much better would the world be if we all pulled in the same direction, shared our resources, looked after one another? Harry had his pack, that was his sanctuary, with people he trusted, they looked after one another, but the ideal of the whole world getting along together could not be achieved. Homo-sapiens were designed to be competitive, a survivor, and as such would always be aggressive, even with his own kind.

FORTY-SIX

What he did was wrong in the eyes of the law, but by ridding the planet of these people he did society a favour. Admittedly, most of society were outside his pack, but not Brian, and that justified the means. The same as in Kuwait all those years ago. He had no choice but to kill those soldiers or he would have been the one to die, and although he enjoyed the killing and the feeling of power, it was a gift he mustn't abuse.

His mind went back to the day he left Kuwait.

ooOoo

The Iraqis had pulled out. Every possible vehicle they could lay their hands on, commandeered, and they fled. So much for Saddam's 'Mother of all Battles'. The much vaunted Republican Guard were on the run. Over a hundred thousand troops, all trying to get away. Thick, black smoke filled the otherwise blue sky; sabotaged oil wells ablaze, millions of gallons of oil released into the waters of the Gulf. Breathing became difficult. Harry pulled his gutra across his face, the cloth helping to filter out some of the smoke.

"Looks like we're in for a long walk, Kalb."

The young dog wagged its tail.

He'd hardly taxed his brain thinking of a name to call the young animal, settling on the Arabic word for dog straight away.

The dog kept him company, possibly even sane over the last month. No way would he abandon it to its fate. No, the dog would come with him.

South seemed to be the obvious direction to go, back towards the Saudi border.

They walked in the choking smoke for over three hours before a Humvee approached, looking menacing as it emerged from gloom; the fifty calibre machine gun remained trained on him the whole time. This was the first allied vehicle he had seen, although he heard helicopters all around him. How on earth they operated in all that smoke he would never know, it was bad enough here on the ground. The vehicle stopped and a young US marine officer stepped out, keeping his M9 pistol pointing in Harry's general direction. He held up his hand for Harry to stop then pointed to the black bag slung over Harry's shoulder.

"Madha yujad fi alhaqiba" What's in the bag?

"As-salām 'alaykum to you too." How are you? "Property of Her Majesty's armed forces and none of your business."

Harry smiled at the officer.

"Identify yourself."

"Fielding, Sergeant, P041629Z, and stop pointing that fucking pistol in my face...Sir."

The officer, clearly taken aback by the response from this scruffy beggar asked Harry to show some form of identification.

"Oh aye, just a minute, my passport and ID are in here somewhere along with my dog tags. Oh, no, wait a minute. I guess I left them with my unit, BECAUSE I'VE BEEN BEHIND ENEMY LINES, YOU FUCKWIT,... Sir."

The officer stood transfixed for a moment then burst into laughter.

"Soldier, after that outburst, you couldn't be anything but a Limey. Where you headed?"

"Somewhere where I can find a decent bloody cup of tea and a bacon sarnie."

The officer motioned for him to wait and returned to the Humvee. After a brief conversation on the radio he called Harry over.

"You got yourself a ride back to HQ, soldier."

Harry smiled. A ride was always better than walking.

FORTY-SIX

"The dog comes with me though."

Harry saw the hesitation on the officer's face.

"The dog comes or we both walk."

Reluctantly, the officer nodded his agreement.

After a few kilometres travelling along Highway 51, one of the other marines turned to Harry.

"Be a mighty fine thing if you or the dog took a shower too, when you get back."

Harry grinned and gave him the 'V', the soldier grinned in return. He was part of Harry's pack.

ooOoo

Truth be told, he still yearned for those days, as dangerous as they were; not for the killing or even the danger, though adrenalin was a drug like any other and some craved it more than others. What he really missed; being part of being something much bigger, belonging, having a purpose.

He lay on his bed and began clearing his mind, shutting down the extraneous thoughts, the white noise of living, until he could concentrate. Maybe he should lay off the killings for a while. Five murders in such a short time drew a great deal of attention; six if you counted Brian. The increase in police activity was evident everywhere and it was getting more and more difficult to move around unseen.

He would allow the trail to go cold and the murders slip from the minds of the public, then start afresh. No one hurt his pack.

CHAPTER FORTY-SEVEN

James wasn't quite sure why he agreed to come in for a night cap.

At least that's what he told himself because deep inside his mind lay the real reason. He was a man; she, a very attractive lady and he loved her company.

She shushed him to be quiet, making more noise than he in the process, as she tried to put the key in the lock. Finally, she succeeded and the two of them giggled their way into Helene's apartment.

As Helene turned to close the door behind them she stumbled against him. Whether caused by the drink, or deliberate he didn't know, nor did he care. The kiss came quickly; slow and lingering in its delivery. All at once they were tearing at each other's clothes. No longer caring. The desire that had been building for years, now found a way to be released.

The contrast of the white pants against her smooth black skin, caused James to pause for a moment. Then they were gone, cast aside, as he immersed himself in a wave of lust and passion, savouring her scent and taste.

It didn't take long for them to move to the bedroom.

FORTY-SEVEN

The lust satisfied; the tenderness yet to come.

Sometime later, laying in the darkness, James said,

"Talk to me in that sexy Jamaican accent."

"Wat tings yah wanting me to say den?"

"Oh, I could listen that all night."

"Maybe yah cud, but dis girl ain't staying up aal night, yah hear?"

She let out a little laugh.

"And I doubt you could too," she added.

They dissolved into fits of giggles, the type that can only be found after alcohol.

CHAPTER FORTY-EIGHT

What was it about crooks that made them want to meet on waste ground? If you want to draw attention to yourself, set up a meeting somewhere out of the way and be the only people there. Far better to meet somewhere public and no one would take the slightest bit of notice. Smoke blamed it on all those American cop programmes; meeting under Brooklyn Bridge in New York, or the Golden Gate in San-Francisco; a scrap of land full of rain filled holes as the villain's car bounced its way to the meeting point. He wouldn't mind if he was somewhere as glamorous as that but where was he? The East End of London; hardly had the same ring to it did it?

At least he took precautions, this top dog. He'd not given Smoke a meeting place directly but moved him from call box to call box until he finally gave directions to this piece of land off the North Woolwich Road, close to the Thames Barrier.

Smoke knew no-one followed him, but he couldn't be sure about the other guy. Still, given the precautions he took in getting Smoke here, he assumed he would be as smart with his own arrival.

FORTY-EIGHT

He left Gypsy behind at the flat. He needed the seat to strap down the four packages. Besides, anyone else there who didn't need to be, would make the guy nervous and Smoke didn't want to scare him off. He needed to make this work.

Holy shit. There's nothing like keeping a low profile when doing a deal, and this was nothing at all like keeping a low profile. The latest Bentley Mulsanne was hardly the most appropriate vehicle to bring to a clandestine meeting, especially in this part of the London. Why the hell did he not come in a Ford Fiesta or something? Anything not to draw attention. If he was trying to impress Smoke, it wasn't working. Apart from the run around in getting here, everything else smacked of 'amateur.'

A goon in a dark suit got out from the front of the car and came to where Smoke leaned against his Triumph, having a cigarette.

The dark suit motioned for him to stand up and spread. Smoke complied and let the guy frisk him thoroughly, a little too intimately for his liking, but it showed a serious commitment to security, even if the Bentley didn't.

The suit turned to the car and gave a single nod. Clearly having been given a signal of some sort that Smoke didn't see, the suit ushered him into the back of the Bentley.

Twenty minutes later Smoke held a bag containing seven hundred and fifty grand and the man in the Bentley had 4 keys of top grade white.

Deal concluded, Smoke returned to his motorcycle and was busy strapping the bag to the seat when all hell broke loose. Four armed response units and three Police minibuses arrived at the entrance to the waste land blocking off the only viable vehicle exit. Smoke made a dash for the river but found himself facing officers from the River Police Unit.

He frantically looked around for a way out but couldn't see anywhere that didn't have a black clad officer running towards him. Knowing when to give up, he sank to his knees and put his hands on his head.

CHAPTER FORTY-NINE

Helene studied herself in the mirror. Not a pretty sight. Pulling her eyelids down, she looked at each blood shot eye in turn. Her mascara was everywhere; the rat's nest on her head the result of frenetic activity in the hall and the bedroom. You are such a slut, she thought to herself.

She looked back at the bed; James no longer there. She vaguely remembered him leaving at some point during the night. It was all a bit of a blur. Too much alcohol and too much sex.

She knew it was a way of letting off steam. Usually, some poor unsuspecting guy she fancied found himself taking her home for the night. In the morning, out she would go, both satisfied and she would never call the inevitable phone number scrawled on a piece of paper.

This time it was a colleague, a married one at that. She hoped he didn't get the wrong idea, think this would lead somewhere, an affair, or heaven forbid, him leaving his wife. No, that would not happen. It wouldn't have happened before, and certainly not now. She couldn't afford to be involved with anyone at this moment.

She had another briefing to attend this morning.

FORTY-NINE

Another body, another briefing. When would it all end? Not until they caught the killer, and so far they had so little to go on. They needed to catch a break. The one piece of the puzzle that would allow all the others to drop into place.

She shook her head vigorously. She had to stop having these late nights. She couldn't be functioning at one-hundred per-cent on so little sleep. That would be it; tonight she would stay in with a bottle of wine, a Chinese take-away, a chick-flick on the movie channel, then an early night.

Thank goodness for the power shower. Not feeling the brightest most mornings, and this being worse than usual, the shower did its job and brought her back to a semi-human state. The morning coffee grabbed from Costa would do the rest.

CHAPTER FIFTY

That should not have happened; unethical, immoral, and so damned good he would do it over and over again.

James closed his eyes and sought out the mental image of the sleeping Helene MacKay he so recently left. Even in the back of the taxi he could still smell her, taste her, feel her.

He had known he was attracted to her. He was male after all; men were designed to be attracted by women, that's how the species survived. What he never expected was to act on that attraction, or how strong it would turn out to be. Certainly there had been lust involved, but it seemed to go far deeper than that. He felt the connection on a mental level, not just physical. Perhaps it was the alcohol, or knowing his marriage on the verge of derailment. Derailment? Ha! A major rail disaster would be more like it if Beth ever found out about this.

He still loved his wife, or at least he thought he did, but it was clear they couldn't live together. They argued most of the time about the inconsequential things. They seemed to be at each other's throats day and night. They had grown apart. People's taste in food and music changed, as indeed ones' taste's in most things changed as one grew older, so why was it expected you would pick a partner for life, and at a relatively early age?

He would need to sleep on it, put things in perspective. He couldn't throw away his marriage on a whim, and he didn't know for sure how Helene felt, or if she would be interested in continuing. He'd heard the rumours, nothing concrete, but there were whispers she liked young athletic men. If so, what on earth would she see in him? He didn't qualify as young, although he kept reasonably fit.

Best thing to do would be to leave things alone and see how it panned out. Maybe when Beth came back from her parents, things would be a little bit different.

He sighed. Who was he kidding? It took two to make a marriage work and only one of them seemed to be employed in this one.

He groaned as he checked the time, 3 AM and a PM to perform when he got in. There would be just enough time for him to sleep long enough to feel really shitty when he got up. Great.

CHAPTER FIFTY-ONE

Chief Superintendent Brandon stormed past the startled officers and out of the door at the far end of the room.

"MacKay, my office, now."

Helene left her room and followed.

Two of the detectives exchanged looks.

"I would bet my last quid she's going to get a lecture on women and the force," said DS Barnes.

"He's not exactly supportive of non-whites either is he?"

"I'd love to be a fly on the wall if he tries that on with her." He raised his eyebrows and tapped his lips with a pencil. "The thing is, she's damned good. Got the best clean up rate in the Met It's just this one is proving difficult, no one sees anything and hey presto, up pops another body."

DS Barnes' colleague shrugged his shoulders, "I'm just a foot soldier, Sarge, I do as I'm told."

"And that, my son, is why you are still a DC."

ooOoo

FIFTY-ONE

"What's happening with these murders? The Commissioner is all over my arse. He wants answers and so do I. We can't have bodies turning up everywhere and no results. What the hell are you doing about it MacKay? Why haven't you made an arrest?"

Helene knew the Superintendent understood exactly what was happening and where they were with the case. He had a briefing every morning. This was him kicking the cat because he'd had a boot up the backside.

"Sir, you know full well we haven't any leads to go on. No one has seen anything in the vicinity of any of..."

"I don't want bloody excuses, I want results. If you are not 'man enough' for the job, I'll put someone on it who is."

"Are you implying I'm not capable of doing my job... Sir?"

The Chief Superintendent didn't believe women were capable of doing what he considered a 'man's job', despite the results she obtained.

"Oh grow up MacKay."

"Or is it because I'm black?"

Helene winced as the words come out of her mouth. How often had she heard this on the street? How often had some little scrote, caught red-handed, uttered that very line, and now she'd said the same.

She watched the Superintendent change from his normal ruddy colour to a Royal Purple.

"Get the fuck out of my office MacKay and get me some results, now. And whilst you're out there, start looking for a new line of work."

Without a word Helene turned and stormed out of the door, swung it hard behind her and at the last moment closed it gently. That would really piss him off.

"Arsehole," she muttered as she went back to her desk,

ignoring the looks of the officers she passed.

ooOoo

Barnes raised his eyebrows at the young DC on the other side of the desk and shook his head.

"I think he just tried it, and we didn't need to be the fly on the wall," he whispered. "Best we go out and do some 'enquiring' whilst we still have our testicles."

Discretion being the better part of valour, the two officers quietly retrieved their jackets and left the room.

HARRY

CHAPTER FIFTY-TWO

She no longer recognised the person staring back from the mirror. Thank goodness for quality makeup; it covered a multitude of sins. She smiled at her own joke, there were some sins makeup would never be able to cover. She glanced at the figure sleeping soundly, half under the duvet on the bed behind her. Another poor unfortunate soul who would wait for the phone call. How long would it be before he realised Helene would not be calling him? She didn't even know his name. A night on the town, an itch that needed scratching and along comes man with no name, bursting with testosterone. The outcome inevitable; borne out by the fact he was in her bed. Not for much longer though, she had a morning briefing to attend and with a series of murders on her hands all of which had become political, she must be on top of her game. She smiled again. She'd been on top of something, that was for sure. She took another glance. He certainly had a body on him, she'd give him that.

"Come on. Off your backside. You've got five minutes. That's all it takes me to put this war paint on."

The sleeping figure groaned, rolled over, and pulled

the crumpled duvet over his head. Helene yanked it off him and dropped it on the floor.

"Now."

He mumbled. "I'm tired. Come back to bed."

"And I'm a Police Officer, now up and out of my flat."

His eyes shot open at the mention of the word Police. He sat there for a moment then his body caught up with his brain and he scrabbled around for his clothes. The last Helene saw of him was as he hopped out of the door, still trying to put on one shoe.

As much as she knew it was wrong, she couldn't help herself. And why shouldn't she? She was single, attractive and solvent.

She knew why she shouldn't. She was punishing herself and she was punishing them. Why she should punish herself she didn't know. She didn't end it but she had been the one to feel the pain of it. She was at a loss to explain why she felt the need to inflict even more pain on herself. Maybe a psychologist could tell her. Perhaps she blamed herself for the break up. Whatever it was, she needed to stop it, but as long as she still got the thrill from the sex, she didn't see how that would happen. As for them, they were men. That was the only excuse she needed to punish them. She hurt, and so would they. If she rationalised it, she realised they were not to blame. They didn't even know her, but just now that didn't make any difference. She had her needs, and she would fulfil them, if someone got hurt in the process, well hard luck.

Out of the corner of her eye she spotted the business card she had been given a week ago. She picked it up from her dressing table. Michael Strong, and a phone number, nothing else. He was attractive enough, she remembered, but this was strictly business. A golden rule, never to be broken; do not mix business with pleasure. She had already broken one golden rule by bringing a stranger back to her apartment, something she had vowed never to do; what on earth had she been thinking.

Her mind went back to yesterday and her brief encounter with the Chief Superintendent. Six months ago he transferred in from SO17 in Westminster. Since then not only had he been a thorn in her side, but he seemed to go out of his way to berate the better officers, almost as if he couldn't tolerate their success. With her clear-up rate she became number one target; always questioning her ability as a female officer and suggesting she only achieved promotion because of her gender and her ethnicity; nothing more. At first Helene put it down to him testing her, but recently it seemed to have become personal, to the point where she was taking Michael Strong's proposal seriously. She never thought she would consider leaving the Met, but then she never believed she would ever meet someone like Chief Superintendent Brandon.

She smiled as she once again thought of Michael Strong. He may well be the cause of another violation of her rules. She cocked her head to one side and smiled again.

ooOoo

Not a bad night's work if I do say so myself, thought Carl as he stumbled down the stairs, tucking his shirt into his jeans. Not the sort of job that comes your way every day, that's for sure. He'd been briefed on similar jobs of course, that's what he was good at; attracting women and luring them into indiscretion. This one turned out to be different, she did all the luring, in fact, she did everything. He'd never come across a woman so wild between the sheets before, and what a woman; not young but a total stunner nonetheless. Anyway, with age comes experience and he certainly learned a thing or two last night. He thought he knew everything; now he knew everything plus some more.

Such a pity it would never happen again. A one-night stand and no more, those were the rules. Never mind, plenty more fish in the sea they say, but when you have just tasted caviar, it's hard to go back to a diet of herring.

That was last night, and this is now. Time to report in and let them know that apart from her being fantastically hot in bed, he had nothing to report. She told him nothing, apart from her being a copper; not exactly a state secret. No pillow talk other than what one would expect to hear in the circumstances.

His masters would be so disappointed. He grinned. Hell, he wasn't.

With a fresh spring in his step, Carl went on his way to meet his contact.

CHAPTER FIFTY-THREE

" Vecuronium bromide."

"And good morning to you too, James."

This was the first time they'd spoken to each other since the night they slept together. To Helene's surprise the sound of his voice raised thoughts in her head; thoughts she never imagined would be there again, thoughts she should not be having about this man. He's married for heaven's sake. She should stay well away from the married ones. She didn't need or want the hassle, and she certainly didn't want to be responsible for the break-up of someone's marriage. There were plenty of unattached fish in the sea.

Suddenly, none of the other fish seemed to be as attractive as this one and she realised that over the years, her feelings towards him had developed into something much stronger than a mild interest. Go on, admit it girl, you've fallen in love. There, said it now. And isn't that typical, of all the men to fall in love with, this one is off limits. That just about summed up her life; didn't want what she could have and couldn't have what she wanted.

"Sorry, good morning, Helene. You were right. She

FIFTY-THREE

screened positive for vecuronium bromide. It's used in theatre as a muscle relaxant. Whoever did this wanted her to suffer because it doesn't act as a pain killer. In layman's terms it's a paralysing agent. So she would have felt the pain and would have been unable to do anything about it."

"Shit. She must...I mean, the needle. Oh god I wouldn't wish that on my worst enemy. So does this mean we are looking for a medical professional?"

Doctor Melbourne took some moments to answer.

"There's a strong possibility. After the results came back I took another look at the body. There were signs of oedema to the bronchial tract which at first I put down to the use of the ligature, but I'm not so sure now. I think she may have been intubated. Without the vecuronium she would be able to fight back, once the vecuronium was administered she would have no muscle control, including, ultimately her breathing, unless whoever did this was very skilled at giving the correct dosage. By intubating, this guy kept her alive so she could suffer the agony. If we are not looking at a medical professional we are definitely looking at someone with a certain amount of medical knowledge, at least paramedic level I would say."

Helene shifted the phone to her other ear. Being left-handed and using her left ear for the telephone made things a little awkward when she wanted to write notes. She scribbled down the relevant details.

"How easy would it be to obtain this ...vec...vecuronium?"

"Not that easy. It will be in hospitals of course but I wouldn't think it would be that easy to come by elsewhere. It's used in the States for the execution of prisoners and the military would use it too."

There it was again, military. They hadn't turned up any links to Hamilton in their enquiries with the MOD but that didn't mean no link exists. There was still the possibility the Army were not telling them everything. It was too much to be co-incidence. Hamilton was ex-military and so were a few of the rough sleepers. Had one of them taken it on themselves to take revenge for his death?

"James, about..."

"Helene, I don't think we should go there. Not at the moment. My head isn't in a good place right now."

So he had been thinking about it too, otherwise how would he know what she wanted to say?

"No. You're right. Well, thank you for the info. I think you may just have done it again, Sherlock."

"Really?"

"You've given me an idea I need to pursue. I'll catch up with you soon."

She hung up before James replied. She was afraid she would give herself away if she spoke to him any longer. She couldn't be sure if she felt vulnerable, lonely or genuinely in love. Whatever it was there couldn't be a future there, or could there? She re-ran what he said about his head not being in the right place. What did he mean by it? If she thought about it too much she would over analyse things and then probably make a fool of herself. She better concentrate on the task in hand and find the person responsible for these murders.

Her first job would be to go to the evidence room. There was something there she needed to take a second look at.

HARRY

CHAPTER FIFTY-FOUR

He stopped his mumblings and took in his surroundings. He had wandered into Stratford, near the Olympic site. He cursed the Olympics. He lost many of his usual sleeping places, and the Police moved on the rough sleepers nightly. It wouldn't do for some visiting athlete or dignitary to see that Britain too had its social problems. Oh no, sweep that one under the carpet and pretend all is well on the western front. Never mind. Now all of the fuss was over things had gone back to normal - almost.

The area around the Olympic site was still sterile as far as he was concerned. Not many opportunities to kip down there without some smart arse copper waking him up in the middle of the night and asking if he didn't have somewhere else to go. Still, he knew a couple of places nearby where he could get his head down for the night. He shuffled along the High Street in the direction of Bow; vaguely aware of people stepping aside, not wanting to be near him. That was their problem. His problems were always the same, where to get the next meal and where to find a decent night's kip, every day a fight for survival.

CHAPTER FIFTY-FIVE

She'd never been to this place before. Something of an oddity as far as coffee shops were concerned. Whoever heard of a coffee shop with a recording studio? When you thought about it, it made perfect sense, coffee and musicians go together as well as coffee and cream. Shoreditch Grind combined the two; a coffee shop downstairs, and an upstairs studio.

The place was far enough from the police station for it to be unlikely she would meet anyone from work. She didn't want to have to explain who the handsome man was approaching her table, and handsome he certainly was. She rose to greet him with a handshake. His grip firm, the pale blue eyes making eye contact with her for just a fraction longer than she found comfortable.

"DCI MacKay, a pleasure to meet you again."

She smiled.

"I suppose you are wondering what this is all about, the cloak and dagger meeting, the request to keep it quiet from your superiors."

Helene smiled again, cocked her head to one side and raised her eyebrows.

FIFTY-FIVE

He returned the smile.

"A woman of few words, I like that. Let's get down to business. We have had our eye on you for quite some time. That's an impressive clear-up rate. You don't suffer fools gladly and you are immensely frustrated when the CPS drops what to you is an open and shut case, for lack of evidence."

"You haven't told me anything I don't already know, Mr Strong."

"Please, call me Michael."

"Well, Michael, who exactly is 'We'?"

Michael continued. "You are single with no family ties, so you would be able to 'disappear' for long periods without arousing suspicion. No steady boyfriend, but a string of, shall we call them 'suitors', the latest last night, at your apartment."

Helene could feel the colour rising in her cheeks.

"Fuck you, Mister. It's none of your damned business who I sleep with, or when."

Michael took a long sip of his espresso. All the while he maintained eye contact, with Helene.

At this time of day, the coffee shop was relatively quiet but they were far enough from the other customers for them not to hear Helene's anger. She suspected the location had been carefully vetted beforehand. If they knew all about her before making the approach, they would certainly have not picked a meeting place at random; whoever 'they' were. After several seconds of Helene glaring at him, he carried on.

"We must be absolutely sure about our recruits, Detective. We rely on being able to operate in secret and we can't afford to bring in the wrong person. Our whole operation would be jeopardised."

"Just who the hell are you?"

Michael steepled his fingers and put them to his lips.

He chose his next words with care.

"Let's say we're doing the exact same job as you, but without the constraints, and once in a while we do a little bit more. We answer to the same masters, but they would deny our existence if word got out."

Helene studied his face. As well as being handsome, he was one cool customer. Not one bit of emotion crossed his face so far. If this was the calibre of people she would be working with, then moving should be something she should consider. She loved her team and what they achieved, but she felt she was being stifled by that misogynistic, racist, bastard of a Superintendent, not to mention all the garbage being thrown their way from Whitehall.

She wondered what he meant by 'lack of constraints', and doing 'a little bit more'. She had her suspicions, and although a strong advocate of due process, she sometimes felt it got in the way of their real job; catching the bad guys. Not the minor drug dealers and burglars, but the organised crime syndicates and drug barons. The people who seemed to be Teflon coated. No matter what the police did to catch them, they somehow always managed to wriggle free. It would be a refreshing change to tackle them head on without having one hand tied behind your back. As long as the evidence was sound.

"And where do I fit into all this?"

"I was hoping that would be your next question."

CHAPTER FIFTY-SIX

Emma concentrated on the figures on the screen. With the EU referendum getting ever closer she must forecast the possible ramifications of a vote for the UK to leave the European Union. While most in her position thought it unlikely, she had a feeling it might not be so clear cut. A leave vote would create a climate of uncertainty and no doubt the pound would lose ground against all the major currencies. The model she worked on aimed to minimise the banks' exposure in such a case. Emma snatched the ringing phone from its cradle; the interruption most unwelcome. The manager would like to see her in his office right away. She did a mental backtrack to review her recent work, and couldn't remember anything out of the ordinary so it was probably nothing to worry about. Maybe she would be getting a bonus, she was good at what she did, often forecasting things others missed. Perhaps they were recognising it.

She tapped on the door of Mr Bartlett's office and received a curt 'come' in reply.

Two gentlemen in dark suits sat in front of Mr Bartlett's desk.

FIFTY-SIX

"Ah, Miss Johnson. I understand from these gentlemen that you made a witness statement regarding a...ahem... an occurrence about which you may have some information."

'Yes, Mr Bartlett, I..."

He held up his hand to cut her off.

"No need to fill me in with the details, my dear. They wish to ask you some further questions."

It was clear he wished to be dissociated from the matter. He nodded to one of the men, an indication for him to take up the conversation.

The man remained silent, raised his eyebrows slightly and inclined his head towards the door.

Mr Bartlett frowned for a moment then with a sudden clarity took the hint.

"Ah..um...yes...err...gentlemen, I have other business to attend to so I will take my leave for a moment. Will you be long, or require refreshments?"

Emma smiled. She didn't deal with Mr Bartlett very often, but when she did she thought him to be a character straight off the pages of a Dickens novel. Even down to the waistcoat and pocket watch. This image of Victorian bankers is what drew her to a career in finance in the first place. Sadly, long been replaced with young movers and shakers; nothing gentlemanly in the banking industry any more.

The one who gestured shook his head. Obviously the more senior of the two.

"Thank you, but no. We'll be brief, Mr Bartlett."

Mr Bartlett digested the information, gave a curt nod and left the room.

"So, gentlemen, how can I be of assistance?" Emma asked, realising she mirrored Mr Bartlett's way of speaking.

One of the dark suits stood.

HARRY

"Emma Johnson, I'm arresting you on suspicion of contravening sections one, two, and three of the Computer Misuse Act Nineteen-Ninety. You do not have to say anything. But it may harm your defence if you do not mention, when questioned, something which you rely on in court. Anything you do say can be given in evidence. This arrest is being been made to allow the prompt and effective investigation of the offences."

The colour drained from her face.

"Do you understand why you've been arrested?"

She stared at her shoes then slowly nodded.

"Okay, Emma, or should I say 0rchid. There are two ways we can do this. One is I put you in handcuffs and march you out of here in front of everybody. The other is that you promise not to make a break for it, we walk out of here, and I tell Mr Bartlett you are accompanying us to the station to look at some mugshots."

Emma staggered and sank into the chair the officer vacated moments ago; her breathing rapid and shallow and her face now flushed.

Her mind rushed over all the steps she took both entering and once inside the GCHQ computer. She couldn't think of one mistake she made. She was certain her technique was flawless.

Emma realised the officer was speaking to her.

"So which is it to be?"

She looked at him with something approaching defiance.

"Which do you think?"

He smiled. "Good girl."

Emma narrowed her eyes. The man didn't behave like a copper, not that she'd met many; he seemed relaxed, informal somehow.

"Can I see your warrant card?" She paused. "Both of you."

FIFTY-SIX

His smile changed to a grin. "Oh you're a very good girl. Trust no one, question everything. I think you'll be just fine."

Emma ran over that sentence in her mind. She could make no sense of why he would say that. Be fine, how, where?

They both showed her their warrants cards and to Emma they looked legit, although she had never seen an actual warrant card before, it did have their pictures and a government crest. She handed them back without a word. Had she paid more attention she might have noticed the absence of the word Police anywhere on the cards.

CHAPTER FIFTY-SEVEN

Today at least, he managed to find a decent meal. He soon learned that some places would give him free food out of pity, and some to get him to leave. The kebab shop was one of the former. Whenever he went near they would always make sure he left with a bag full of food. The Iraqis running the kebab shop were more of a friend to him now than most of his own people.

One thing that almost all the politicians had in common; they failed to realise how out of touch they were with the real world. The real people of the country were struggling for survival. Being broke to the people was about not having enough money to pay the prescription charges, not being able to pay the rent unless they missed a meal or two, not having enough food to feed all of the family, and in some cases, not even having a roof over their heads. Being broke was not about having to postpone buying the house in the country, or having to make an expenses claim off the taxpayer because the moat needed cleaning. Their lack of understanding of the real world was allowing society to break down; to lose its discipline. People no longer cared about each other, they only cared about survival.

The Old Man wandered into the small churchyard of St Mary-atte-Bow. The church was an island in a river of traffic. Being surrounded on both sides by a road meant he was less likely to be disturbed by passers-by. Only troublemakers or PC Plod would disturb him and as it meant getting out of the nice comfy car he doubted that Plod would bother. He settled on the bench nearest the church door for the night. At least he didn't need the newspapers anymore. A lovely evening promised to turn into a balmy night. Perfect for sleeping in the open. What more could a man ask for?

CHAPTER FIFTY-EIGHT

As she left the bank in the company of the two men, Emma once again felt something didn't quite fit. The one who arrested her, 'Boss' as she now thought of him, spoke to Mr Bartlett as they were leaving and he seemed unusually quiet for someone who was about to lose an employee for a number of hours. Trying to arrange time off for anything here almost required a Papal decree, and yet here he was, as meek as a mouse letting her take time off to help the police with their enquires. Then there was the car. She didn't think the police were in the habit of driving around in black E Class Mercedes.

As the car made a U-turn and set off in the direction St Paul's Cathedral, she assumed they were taking her to New Scotland Yard to be interviewed. That's where they took all the serious criminals as far as she remembered, although she wasn't sure. She'd never been involved with the police before.

She put her head in her hands. She was so sure she wouldn't be caught; her code flawless. How on earth did they find out? She wanted excitement and now she'd found it; in buckets.

FIFTY-EIGHT

Emma frowned as she gazed out of the car window. She turned to the 'Boss' sitting beside her.

"Where are we going?"

The car continued along Abingdon Street past the Palace of Westminster, otherwise known as the Houses of Parliament; already beyond the turn to Scotland Yard.

"Legoland."

"But that's out at Windsor and you wouldn't..." She stopped speaking; he didn't mean that Legoland.

"You mean the SIS building, don't you?" She referred to the not-so-secret, Secret Intelligence Services building, which amongst its many names boasted Legoland as one of them.

"They said you are a smart girl."

She lapsed back into silence. This was more serious than she ever imagined it would be. She knew the law. As long as she didn't do anything except look, then she would probably receive a fine, but once national security came into it, they could put her away for life. All kinds of scenarios flashed through her mind.

She might be made to disappear. She dismissed that one. If they were going to make her disappear, they wouldn't take her from her place of work in full view of everyone. She would vanish from her flat in the middle of the night, and no one would ever know where she went. No, as serious as this was, she didn't think she would be 'terminated with extreme prejudice', as they liked to call it, according to the movies anyway.

Ten minutes later they pulled into the car park beneath the iconic building of the Secret Intelligence Services, often referred to as MI6.

Emma exited the car and promptly threw up. What had she done?

ooOoo

She found herself being ushered into an underground office. Simple but functional furniture adorned the room. Nothing like the grandiose and sumptuously decorated office Mr Bartlett occupied. But then he was a senior in a bank, and this a government department. She suspected the ministers would enjoy better furniture.

She was told to take a seat and someone would be along shortly to discuss her future. The way he said it sounded like she had one, but she couldn't see how. These were serious allegations and they wouldn't bring her here to smack her wrists and tell her not to do it again.

As she waited, she surveyed the room and noted the camera in the corner of the ceiling. No doubt they were watching her right now. She sat back in her chair and examined her fingernails, trying to appear calm.

After what seemed like hours, but in reality was probably five minutes, a tall man entered and sat behind the desk. He didn't look at her but flicked the pages of a dossier on the desk, scanning down each one. He reached the last page, sighed, carefully placed the folder squarely on the desk, lifted his head and smiled.

This was the first time Emma had met anyone with eyes as blue as hers, and it startled her.

"So, Miss Johnson, or can I call you Emma?"

She nodded, not trusting herself to speak just yet. She would probably squeak, or at the least have a tremor in her voice. Now was not the time to show weakness.

"Emma, my name is Michael. You do realise you are facing some serious charges here? You could go to prison for life."

"I didn't do anything. I only..."

She stopped. Oh, very clever.

"On the contrary, Emma, you broke through some of the toughest security in the world and gained access to a highly sensitive and classified computer system. A system that cost this country an absolute fortune to create, yet you

FIFTY-EIGHT

accessed it with a home computer."

Emma thought about her set-up; home computer was not quite how she would describe it, but she conceded his point.

"A system containing many secrets, which if exposed would be a major blow to national security."

He let the sentence float like a wisp of smoke in the room.

She'd seen this technique used in some TV programme or other. Stop speaking, let the suspect sit in silence, make them feel uncomfortable, and they'll want to fill the void with their own sound. She wouldn't fall for it.

"You are very good. Even now you are giving nothing away, just like you didn't when you broke into the computer. Not a trace of you."

"There must have been something or I wouldn't..."

She stopped. She walked right into that one didn't she?

Michael kept eye contact with her, until she had to turn away.

"I can assure you no trace existed at GCHQ, however we do have evidence you were the perpetrator. Look, you might as well talk about it, because we have enough to put you away until you are an old lady, and I'm sure prison would be no place for someone like you."

Emma took a deep breath, weighed up the consequences and made her decision.

"Okay, I admit it. I did it, but I didn't do anything. I just wanted to know I could do it."

"So did we, Emma, so did we."

She was puzzled; the interview not going the way she expected, not in the slightest.

"You said I didn't leave a trace and I'm sure you couldn't track back, so how did you know it was me?"

Michael picked up the phone on his desk and

summoned someone into the room. Moments later a skinny male, wearing thick, black rimmed glasses entered. Far too young to be in a place like this, she thought.

"Emma, I believe you know this young man?"

She frowned and shook her head.

"I don't think..."

The newcomer smiled, almost apologetically.

"Hello, 0rchid, I'm Jack Sparrow."

Emma gasped, flushed, then went cold, her emotions galloping like a two-year old colt.

Michael continued.

"When 'Jack' here sent you the code, he sent you something else too. We gambled on you being so keen to receive the code, you wouldn't spot the extra in the zip file. We knew you were good; how good remained to be seen. The little extra package we slipped in has allowed us to monitor all your keystrokes ever since then. We know everything about you."

Emma's eyes widened for a moment.

"Yes, that too."

It was if Michael read her mind. Maybe he could, perhaps they planted code there too. She felt the anger rising. An unwritten code existed amongst coders, even though that was contradictory; they didn't rat on each other. There had to be trust somewhere.

She turned to 'Jack' and gave him a piece of her mind. Both he and Michael let her have her say. When she finished 'Jack' was the first to speak.

"Yes, you are right, and I'm sorry, but, I was a hacker once too; still am I suppose. I had an unfortunate piece of bad luck and got caught, just like you. Michael here gave me the option of spending a number of years in prison, and as you can probably imagine prison would not be the ideal place for me, or come here and work for the

FIFTY-EIGHT

government, getting paid for something I'd been doing for free. No brainer really."

Emma turned back to Michael as he spoke.

"And that is exactly what we are offering you. That piece of code 'Jack'...oh for goodness sake we might as well use your real name... the piece of code Chris here gave you, was the best we could come up with. You took it, altered it and cracked the defences wide open."

"If you only had a key logger you couldn't know that."

Michael and Chris exchanged glances as if to say, I told you she was smart.

"No. You're right. We installed a camera in your apartment."

Emma's face turned red.

"It's okay, we'll destroy the recordings."

She put her head in her hands. Could it get any worse? She'd been caught red-handed breaking into a government computer, they were aware of her online browsing interests, and now they undoubtedly had film of her and some of her 'friends.'

She rewound the conversation. If she wasn't mistaken he just offered her a job.

"Wait, you want me to work here? Be a spy?"

"No, Emma, you will not be Jane Bond, nor will you have a licence to kill...unlike some," he added under his breath. "You will join a small team working for the government tracking down criminals and obtaining evidence that so far normal methods have been unable to achieve."

He paused briefly.

"I say working for the government, however, the government will never acknowledge your existence. You are single, correct?"

Emma nodded.

"And no close living relatives, or serious relationships? No one who would miss you?"

She thought about her 'friends', none of them anything more than passing acquaintances.

"I think you probably already know. After all, you are the ones with the video."

"Indeed that is so. The work may be dangerous, but I doubt it will ever be dull."

He smiled again at her.

"What do you say then, Emma?"

Emma smiled back.

"You already know that too, don't you?"

CHAPTER FIFTY-NINE

On a hunch, Nicky made his way to the church in Bow High Street, a place favoured by the Old Man, and sure enough the hunch paid off. At the far end of the churchyard, the Old Man occupied the bench nearest church door, tucking into, what appeared to be from this distance, a kebab.

The light faded as the evening drifted away into early night. Even though the sun had gone down it was still warm. Nicky had no worries about the Old Man sleeping out in this. He slept out on far colder nights, wrapping himself in newspapers to fight off the penetrating cold of mid-winter.

Nicky sat beside him and silently handed him the cup of coffee he'd brought from the McDonald's. He brought him a burger too, just in case. The Old Man nodded and grunted as he accepted the coffee from him. He didn't pause in his attack on the kebab, though he found it harder to keep it together in the one hand, so he reached down and put the coffee cup on the floor.

There would be no conversation until he finished eating, so Nicky tucked into his own 99p burger. Not his

FIFTY-NINE

first or even third choice of meals, but something to share a social moment with the old boy.

The Old Man carefully rewrapped the now half-eaten kebab and put it back in the brown paper bag. Clearly he planned on having it for breakfast the following day. Not a prospect Nicky would consider, that's for sure. He had come across many a half-eaten kebab in his kitchen, following a night out on the ale. Certainly not something he could tackle with a hangover, and he doubted he would when cold stone sober either. Still, he could get food when he wanted and the old boy had to get his when he could.

Despite knowing him for a number of years, Nicky knew precious little about him, apart from that he had once been in the forces, as indeed had several of the homeless in London. Other than that, the Old Man had said very little about himself. Where he opened up was when Nicky asked about life on the streets. He hadn't been complimentary about successive governments; people lived and died on the streets, and little if anything ever done about it. Now, with austerity biting hard in every aspect of local government, the number of homeless was on the increase. The Old Man had made no secret of the fact he despised all politicians, most business men, and the majority of the human race in general, for not giving a damn about the plight of their fellow man. He had conceded there were one or two kind souls in the world, and had eventually placed Nicky in that category.

Nicky liked the old boy and his view of the world; not so far removed from his own. And perhaps had it not been for lady luck smiling on him from time to time, he might be living the same life. 'There but for the grace of God' applied to all of us.

Hunger satisfied, the Old Man took a sip of coffee, and screwed up his face.

"You always forget the bloody sugar."

Nicky laughed.

"I do, yes."

"Well, thanks anyway. What brings you here this time of night?"

"Oh, I was just on my way back from giving a talk to a writers' group about the changes in journalism over the years. Thought I'd take a chance and see if you were here."

"Any particular reason?"

"Nope. Just like to make sure you are okay from time to time. Especially with the attacks happening again. Thank goodness, there have been no more deaths, well not any of you guys. Plenty of other bodies turning up it seems."

The Old Man grunted and said, "Not enough of them as far as I'm concerned, but I can look after myself, Lad."

"As cantankerous as ever. I know you can, but some of us do care you know."

The Old Man sighed. "Aye, Lad, and I'm grateful for it. But don't you dare tell anyone I said so."

Nicky smiled. He had taken to this Old Man, as set in his ways as he was.

"I'm afraid I'm no further on with my investigations. I turned up a few right wing groups, but attacks on Asians and blacks is more their style."

"At least you're trying, Lad, that's all I can ask for. More than the bloody police are doing anyway."

Nicky turned towards the Old Man, "You know that's not true. They're doing their best, but with so little to go on."

"And how would you know?"

"Let's just say I have friends in useful places."

The Old Man grunted in response.

The discussion turned to politicians and what makes someone want to 'serve the people'; the Old Man vociferous in his views; the only service any politician did was self-service.

Nicky glanced at his watch.

"I better be on my way, early morning meeting tomorrow. Be a bloody waste of time, they always are. You take care."

The Old Man nodded and said, "Thanks. You are one of the few people I don't mend spending a bit of time with, Lad. You understand."

Nicky waved as he left the churchyard and took the short walk to the railway station.

He remained unaware of the eyes watching from the shadows of the bus shelter across the road. Nor did he notice when a man stepped out and started to follow. After his talk with the Old Man, as usual, Nicky had plenty to occupy his mind.

CHAPTER SIXTY

After leaving the Old Man, Nicky set off back to his apartment in Wapping High Street. There were few people on the streets at this time of night, but he didn't mind. He felt safe. Even though the borough was now full of what his father called 'bloody foreigners', he was still comfortable. This is where he belonged. The opportunity arose on more than one occasion for him to move to somewhere more upmarket, and goodness knows, when he was the editor of the paper he could certainly afford something pretty flashy, but he didn't. He wanted to stay with his roots; where he grew up. His apartment might stretch that definition a little, but he still lived in the same borough where he spent his childhood, and that's what mattered to him.

For some reason Lenny's warning came back to him, 'Munro's out, and he wants revenge.'

Since that night in his apartment, he'd not heard or seen anything from Munro. Maybe he hadn't been there after all. Perhaps he hired a rent-a-thug to put the frighteners on him. It certainly succeeded that night, but the effect wore off as time passed. Nicky wondered why Munro

SIXTY

didn't just wait for him in the apartment, if he wanted revenge. Perhaps the CCTV at the entrance had something to do with it. Quite one thing getting into someone's apartment, but no one in their right mind would kill, knowing CCTV would be the first thing to be checked.

Even so, Munro had taken a chance banking on Nicky not calling the police, but what could he tell them? - Someone broke into my apartment and left me a piece of anchor chain?

He hopped on the Docklands Light Railway at Bow Church and became deep in thought about his conversation with the Old Man and the plight of the homeless. He paid no attention to the other passengers, including the man who followed him from the church and sat a few seats away from him.

Nicky always left the train at Shadwell Station; still about three quarters of a mile away from his apartment, but he didn't mind the walk. Since moving back to London, he hardly used his car. He entered the grandly named Wapping Woods. Presumably it had been woodland long ago, when London was a small community on the Thames, but now only a couple dozen trees and bushes remained, trapped in a forest of brick, glass, concrete and metal.

Nicky's mind returned to the plight of the homeless and whether the problem would ever be solved, when a noise behind caused him to turn.

ooOoo

Gotchya, ya wee bastard, Munro thought as Nicky left the church grounds. This time you are not going to slip through my grasp. Not until I'm good and ready to let your scrawny neck go. I'm going to enjoy watching you die.

He'd started to doubt following the old tramp would ever pay off and thought about giving up trying to track down Rolands that way. Just goes to show you should never quit when you want something. His patience paid off; Rolands was now in his sights.

Munro followed Nicky to the DLR station at Bow Church. It was only a small place so he couldn't very well hide, but he kept his face out of the light, just in case. Nicky seemed oblivious to him anyway, and paid no attention when he sat a few seats away from him on the train.

Assuming he stuck to his normal pattern he would get off at Shadwell and walk through the woods. Well, this will be your last time, Rolands. You won't be walking anywhere after this.

True to form, Nicky came out of the station making a bee-line for the path leading into the woods. Munro would take him at the far end of the block of flats bordering the path; less likelihood of being seen.

The cold steel felt good in his hand. It had been many years since he held a cut-throat razor, too many. In his youth he built up a formidable reputation with one of these, and tonight, this blot on his landscape would find out why.

Intent on his quarry, Munro moved ever closer. He wanted to be in a position to strike, before Rolands made it onto the street. How ironic he would never reach the street he was never meant to return to twenty-six years ago. Rolands had chosen to live within striking distance of Munro's former offices. This time there would be no mistake, Rolands would be out of his life forever.

He raised his right hand in which he held the razor, ready to strike at Rolands' neck and reached forward with his left to grab his hair to pull his head back and expose the throat.

Why did he have a searing pain in his own neck?

Munro's final thought as he was dragged backwards; Ya wee bastard, yous done it again.

SIXTY

ooOoo

Nicky turned in time to see a person being dragged into the trees, frantically clawing at their neck. He wanted to shout but no sound would come, then he did something he could not explain. He moved towards them. As he got closer he recognised the person dragging the writhing and kicking figure deeper into the bushes.

"Lenny, what the...?"

"Keep your voice down, you moron. You want the law around?"

"You're killing him."

Lenny gave Nicky a look that said, 'well spotted.'

The figure on the ground gave a few final kicks then stopped moving. Lenny released the wire he had around his neck.

"Jeez Lenny, is he...?

"You still don't know do you? Take a gander, Nicky boy. Take a good look at his face. Yes, he's dead, because if he wasn't, you would be."

Nicky was shocked to recognise the face of Donald Munro. Prison hadn't been kind to him. His appearance older than his years.

Lenny returned to the path and picked up something from the grass at the side. He held up an open razor to show Nicky.

"This is what he had in his hand. He was about to jump you, Nicky boy."

"How did?...I mean...I don't know what I mean." Nicky felt his knees buckling and he abruptly sat down on the ground.

"Nicky, get off your arse and help me drag him behind that tree. We need to get out of here."

CHAPTER SIXTY-ONE

The Old Man's eyes opened just as the fist aimed at his head started its journey. Time slowed as the adrenaline coursed into his bloodstream. His arm shot out deflecting the blow slightly sideways, the other arm grabbing his assailant's elbow, using the momentum of the punch to pull him towards him. Off balance the attacker fell in front of the bench landing heavily on his right shoulder. The Old Man rolled off the bench onto the dazed figure and was rewarded with a satisfying thud and the sound of air being rapidly expelled from the man's lungs.

A second attacker stood transfixed, baseball bat in hand. The Old Man should be an easy target; this was not supposed to happen. He noticed just a fraction too late the Old Man was on his feet; his knee making contact with his groin. As he doubled in agony the Old Man jabbed his fingers upwards into the attacker's throat, collapsing his trachea. He fell onto the path clutching at his neck, his inability to breathe overcoming the pain in his groin. The Old Man knew he wouldn't be a threat for some time and turned back to the first assailant, watching him struggle to his feet using the bench as support. The Old Man chopped

SIXTY-ONE

hard on the back of his neck, a disabling blow. He searched the now motionless man and found what he expected, a knife. When would they ever learn? He kept the knife in his hand and went back to the man on the path who still gasped for air. Keeping an eye on his face he searched this attacker; the man's eyes full of fear. The Old Man had been an easy target, an old wino sleeping it off; not supposed to fight back but cower whilst they beat him, had a bit of fun. He found a large knife tucked into the back of the man's belt. He shook his head.

"You could hurt someone with this if you are not careful, Son," he said, pocketing the knife, and as he did so he plunged the knife he still held from the first attacker into the side of the man's neck.

"Don't fuck with the SBS, Sonny," he whispered in his ear.

Returning to the man behind the bench, he rolled him onto his back. Taking the second knife from his coat pocket, he thrust it upwards through the diaphragm behind the man's ribcage, aiming for the heart, giving it a twist as he did so.

Now the Police had a double fatal stabbing to solve. Some politician would seek his fifteen minutes of fame and call on the government to rid the streets of these weapons; come down hard on anyone caught carrying a knife. Not that any of them really cared, because they were never on the streets, insulated from the real world by their important positions in society. The police would have a brief purge and then it would be business as usual. They may spend a little longer over this one and surmise these were the two responsible for the death of Brian.

The Old Man took off the latex gloves he wore and dropped them into a carrier bag he retrieved from inside his coat. He would lose them in a bin somewhere on his way. Picking up the bag containing his half-eaten kebab, he shuffled out of the churchyard. He needed to find another bed for the night. Might as well go back to his apartment.

He turned back to look once more at the lifeless bodies of Grease and Jakey and shook his head.

Harry did have a job; he was a street cleaner: just not a conventional one.

CHAPTER SIXTY-TWO

Back at his apartment Nicky poured two large glasses of Scotch, handing one to Lenny.

He dropped himself into an armchair and motioned Lenny to the sofa.

"I think you need to start at the beginning and do some explaining. I just witnessed a murder."

"I told you, Nicky boy. I heard through the grapevine he still lusted for your head. When you left my office, I went to find him; been tailing him ever since. He came to this building once, you know. Tonight he watched you from the bus stop outside St Mary's. He's been following the old geezer you were talking to."

"Why are you keep an eye out for me?"

"Old times' sake I suppose. You were always straight with me at school and we were good mates once. You knew the cops were still on the lookout for Lenny Morvern, you could have told them that he and Leonard Stone, the respectable gemstone dealer were one and the same. You could have given me away; you didn't."

"Why are they still looking for you, Lenny?"

SIXTY-TWO

"How come you never asked me that at the office? Come on, Nicky boy, use that brain. I worked for Munro for a number of years. I was no angel. In any case, they may want back the assets of a certain Mr Munro after I nicked them from under their noses."

Nicky sprayed out his Scotch.

"You took Munro's assets?"

"Yep. How did you think I got to be where I am now?"

Nicky shook his head. "I just assumed... you...well... how the hell did you manage that?"

"You assumed I nicked the stuff, well I did, but not from the nice people. The night of the arrest, I turned up in a Met Police truck with a bunch of hired hands and loaded it all into the back: furniture, money, gems, the lot. Evidence, for safe keeping." Lenny beamed. "And all those years Munro thought I was as thick as two planks."

"How did you know he would be arrested?"

"Nicky boy, who do you think tipped them off about the money?"

"And now you've killed him. I'm not sure I can be a part of that."

"You already are, Nicky boy, you already are. Who's going to cry over Munro, eh? Keep shtum and we'll be ok. Besides, they'll think it's this serial killer. He seems to be going after the villains doesn't he?"

"I don't know, Lenny. Nicking stuff is one thing, but murder? I know he was..." His voice tailed off as he remembered exactly what he was.

"The way I see it is you've no choice, Nicky boy. You helped me move him, you're an accomplice now."

He handed Nicky his empty glass. "How's about a top up, eh?"

CHAPTER SIXTY-THREE

"They fucking what?"

Daniel couldn't believe his ears. He glanced at the tall man standing by the window with his back to the room, before turning his attention back to his boss. He nodded towards the figure still studying the car park through the blinds.

His boss held up a hand and shook his head. A clear indication he was nothing to do with this latest news. To be fair, the head of the HM Customs and Revenue Investigation Unit appeared both embarrassed and annoyed at the news he'd just imparted.

"CPS say there's insufficient evidence they could use in court."

"How the fuck can they say that? We got the guy on camera and on tape. No mean feat I can tell you. They frisked me well. These guys are suspicious, but that's beside the point. We got him buying four kilos of heroin and the CPS say there's not enough evidence? What do they want, the guy to do the deal in front of a judge and sign an affidavit? What the fuck have Katrina and I been doing undercover for the last year if it isn't gathering

SIXTY-THREE

evidence?"

Daniel's boss held up both hands trying to placate him.

"Good morning, Daniel. Michael Strong."

Daniel turned as the tall man held out his hand. He had the bluest eyes he'd ever seen.

"You have me at a disadvantage Mr Strong. You clearly know who I am." The handshake was firm.

The man gestured to a chair. "Please, take a seat."

"I prefer to stand until I know what's going on. Are you CPS?"

The stranger nodded to Michael's boss who left the room without saying another word. The stranger sat newly vacated chair behind the boss's desk. Clearly he was either somebody important, or an asshole. Daniel reserved judgment for the time being.

"I represent some people in government who share your frustrations, Daniel. You, and Katrina have been on our radar for quite some time. Your undercover work is second to none."

He held up his hand as Daniel was about to interrupt.

"Please, let me say my piece, then you can say yours. I don't deal in flattery, if I say you are the best, then that is what I think. As I was saying, your undercover work has impressed us. Your ability, and I am speaking about both of you here, your ability to put yourselves in any situation and blend in without arousing suspicion makes you a valuable asset. No one looking at the smartly dressed man before me now would recognise the hardened biker of a few months ago.

"The people I represent need someone of your calibre. I note your resentment of the CPS to proceed on this case, and I believe it isn't the first. Our aim is to redress the imbalance, which on occasion may require us to work outside the legal framework."

Daniel raised his eyebrows.

"Yes, that statement has raised many more eyebrows than yours. The team we are assembling will discuss each case and how to proceed. At any time, if one of the members does not believe the course of action to be correct, we will reassess and decide how to move forward as a team. We don't aim to be vigilantes. All we are trying to achieve is that which the law sometimes frustrates."

Daniel found himself nodding in agreement to this last statement.

"Of course, you are under no obligation to join us and if you choose to remain here, nothing further will be said."

"You said both of us? I can't speak for Katrina. I would need to talk to her, but I must say the prospect of not having the CPS block everything is a tempting one. I... no...we will need to know far more."

"Yes, you will. A full, no obligation briefing will be given if you agree. You will still be able to walk away at that point; after signing a new copy of the Official Secrets Act, of course. As for Katrina, she already said yes on the condition of you agreeing."

'Has she now?' thought Daniel. Cheeky little madam. She knew that would put pressure on him.

CHAPTER SIXTY-FOUR

St Mary-atte-Bow was a church at peace with itself again. The Police tape denoting the crime scene had been cleared away and the path had been scrubbed. A casual visitor would have no idea of the loss of life that occurred here just two weeks ago. Even had they known, he doubted they would care. Life comes, life goes; the French understood that enough to have a saying; C'est la vie.

Harry knew. He sat two metres away from where he had taken the lives of the two misfits who had the misfortune to attack him. Whether they were the ones who savaged his friend he doubted he would ever find out. Quite frankly, he didn't care. The world had two fewer pieces of flotsam. Would anyone weep? He doubted that too. He closed his eyes, the warm sun making him sleepy. Tilting his head back he let the rays penetrate into the depths of his facial hair.

There was something as equally strange about churchyards as churches, when it came to sound. Although a busy main road passed either side, the noise of the traffic seemed to recede once the grounds were entered. More so than could be accounted for by the

SIXTY-FOUR

shrubbery and trees planted along the railings surrounding the churchyard. Harry had no idea why it should be, but he remained thankful for it. That made St Mary's his favourite place. He came here for peace and solitude, well most of the time anyway. He glanced briefly at the spot where the two attackers had died. C'est la vie.

The sleepiness getting the better of him, Harry dozed in the warmth of another lovely summer's day.

He became aware of someone sitting on the same bench. He kept his eyes closed, though he was curious. No one ever chose to sit next to a homeless person.

"Hello."

He recognised that voice; no mistaking the rich, slightly husky voice of DCI MacKay. One of the few people Harry felt worthy of the time of day. He opened his eyes. She smiled at him. One of the loveliest women he had ever seen, and he'd seen a few in his time.

Harry couldn't help but smile back. Whatever his mood, Helene MacKay always brought out the best in him. There was no side to her. One of the few genuine people in the world, and certainly the only copper he would speak to. She'd always been kind to him. Not the sort of kindness borne by a sense of duty, or because it was the right thing to be seen to be doing. The sort of kindness that only comes from deep within, genuine, real humanity.

She handed him a bag; a Waitrose pasta salad and a doughnut.

"How are you doing?"

"Can't complain detective, and thank you."

He tucked into the pasta.

She let him eat for a while before starting the inevitable discussion about football. That had been the biggest surprise to him as he got to know her; she knew as much about football as any man, pity she was a Chelsea supporter, but then someone had to be, he supposed. And it came as a surprise to many his own team was from the north, Blackburn Rovers. Not in the same league as Chelsea, literally, though they had once been winners of the Premier Division. Always a lively debate ensued about the merits of various players when in the company of DCI MacKay.

Pasta consumed, Harry set about tackling the doughnut.

Helene smiled as he broke off a piece and popped it into his mouth.

"You're good, I'll give you that, Harry."

He stopped chewing. She called him by his name. How did she know his name? He never told anyone his name. She only knew him as Old Man.

"Tell me, how did you manage to avoid being seen all that time?"

He looked at her questioningly and swallowed the piece of doughnut.

"What do you mean?"

Helene opened her handbag and pulled out an evidence bag; inside lay a solitary button. He knew straight away what it was. The question was, how did she know?

"You had me fooled for quite a while, but then little things started to drop into place, like this, and it all started to make sense."

He held her gaze.

"Oh you're good Harry. It is yours isn't it?"

He resisted the temptation to glance down at the buttonhole bereft of its button, now so clearly displayed in the evidence bag.

He kept his face devoid of any emotion, but he knew she knew, and she was a police officer.

ooOoo

SIXTY-FOUR

Helene studied his eyes. He was good indeed. He didn't pat his coat or look down. The average person would have responded immediately and given themselves away, but Harry didn't move a muscle.

"Two from the bottom. That's the missing one."

Harry finally lifted the bottom of his coat to confirm the button was missing.

"It must have come off when I was sleeping somewhere."

Helene cocked her head on one side. "We both know that's not true, Harry. SOCO recovered it from under the body of Ronald Silver. Remember him, the rapist? I'm betting we can match the fibres found on the victim to your trousers, the same fibres we found on the other victims."

For a full minute they sat in silence, looking at each other.

"The two here were yours too weren't they? I wasn't sure at first, a different MO, no ligature marks and no bible passages. What happened, Harry? Did they jump you, or were you waiting for them? The fibres are what gave it all away. When the ones from here matched fibres found at the other scenes, we knew the same person was responsible for all of the deaths. What we still didn't know was who that person was, but we did match the DNA on this button to hairs found at some of the other scenes. I'm betting we'll find that matches yours. That would link you to all of the murders, with the exception of Brian's of course and I'm certain you didn't do that."

Harry stayed silent.

"I must say the church was particularly inventive."

Helene hesitated before she spoke again.

"I'm leaving the Met."

Harry raised his eyebrows.

"It's still difficult being a woman there and, despite the progress, being black doesn't help. So it's time to leave."

"You never struck me as the quitting type." Harry's voice sounded a little shaky.

"Oh, I'm not quitting, I'm moving on. I've been offered a position with some people who can make use of my detective skills. I'm good at what I do, and they recognise it." She paused for a moment. "And I think you are good at what you do too. It's been the devil's own job getting information on you, but I pulled a few strings and called in a few favours. It seems you have an ability we could use."

Harry stared at her.

"I'm not sure what you are saying. Are...are you offering me a job?" He sounded incredulous.

"That depends. We need someone to train field operatives. Someone who knows how to move quietly and invisibly. Someone like you."

"To do what?"

"Let's say this group operates under the radar and are not..." Helene searched for the right words. "...as constrained by the laws of the land as some others maybe?"

"You're going to be a spook?" He raised his eyebrows again.

She laughed and shook her head.

"There are a few villains out there, the really nasty ones, everyone knows are guilty but we just can't gather enough evidence by legitimate methods to prove it. We won't have to follow the rules quite as closely to prove their guilt, but that doesn't mean we have carte-blanche. We still have to satisfy our masters that there's no other way to deal with them."

"But you know now I'm a killer, surely you can't be condoning that?"

SIXTY-FOUR

Helene shrugged.

"Sometimes we may need to take some action that wouldn't be considered... how can I put this...legal?"

Harry shook his head.

"You're doing black ops aren't you? You are going after these guys on a level playing field." He could hardly keep the excitement out of his voice.

"You play by our rules, Harry. No doing your own thing."

"And if I refuse?"

Helene held up the evidence bag.

He let out a roar of laughter.

"Well, I'll be buggered. Out manoeuvred by a copper, and a woman at that." He nodded to the evidence bag.

"What about that?"

"It never existed. The people I work for removed it from the records. They can just as easily put it back again."

"They can do that?"

"You'd be surprised at what they can do."

Harry sighed. His gaze went around the church yard and then to his hands, finally resting back with Helene. He nodded.

"So you'll do it?"

"Too bloody right I will, even if I didn't have a choice."

Helene smiled.

"Oh, and I have a bit of good news for you about Brian's killers."

Harry looked at her questioningly.

Helene pointed at the ground where Jakey and Grease breathed their last.

"Good work, Harry."

CHAPTER SIXTY-FIVE

Helene's excitement was nearing a peak, this the first meeting of the newly formed unit. From the furtive glances being exchanged it was clear that few of the others knew each other. To her right, she hardly recognised Harry; clean shaven and smartly dressed, he was a long way from the image of a rough-sleeping down and out. Whatever Harry had been told in his individual brief, it clearly agreed with him.

Besides herself and Harry she recognised only one other around the highly polished mahogany table. Next to, and in deep conversation with him, another familiar face, although to start with she couldn't quite place him. Early to mid-fifties, a little unkempt and windswept would be the polite way of describing him. She wondered how he knew Harry. That was not the conversation of strangers, too animated, flowing and ebbing as conversations do between friends. Then it dawned on her. He was the newspaper reporter, who gave her a hard time at the press conference. At one time he had been the editor of one of the more respectable papers, this was Nicky Rolands no less. She would be having a chat with him, that was for sure.

SIXTY-FIVE

He glanced across, gave her a nice smile and nodded.

Cheeky sod, after what he said to her, even if he was right. She couldn't help but smile back. It was clear why they chose him for the team. He had a nose for a story and dug up information no other reporters could. He would be an asset to a team whose first role in their investigations would be to gather intelligence

Helene's attention returned to the room they were in. 'Room' seemed to be a grossly inadequate word. A former Victorian Manor house, the table they now gathered around had once seen some of the most sumptuous dinner parties for nineteenth-century London's elite. Walls adorned with enormous portraits reached up to the heavily gilded plaster cornice beyond which, arching majestically over their heads was a richly decorated ceiling. Three large, ornate chandeliers provided illumination. What tales would they tell if they could speak?

She scanned the assembled group. No doubt she would get to know most of them well over the coming years. Nearest to her on her left, four men sat together, not speaking to each other. She suspected they were to be Harry's protégés: rippling muscles, cropped hair and alert manner. Recognising each other for what they were, they had congregated together; safety in numbers. To their left, a young man wearing thick rimmed glasses and looking barely old enough to be out of school, decidedly uncomfortable in the presence of the other four. He drummed his fingers nervously on the table until the man nearest to him reached forward placing his hand on the top of young man's. Message received, he dropped them to his lap, his head bowed to stare at them. Stereotyping, Helene suspected he would be the resident geek and hacker. Beyond him, a slightly older girl sat with the confidence some seem to acquire from birth. Flowing long blond hair, high cheekbones and an air of superiority. This one had Helene stumped. Maybe she was part of the house, the resident Duchess or something. She wondered if the girl was related to Michael; she had the same striking blue eyes.

The remaining couple were nondescript in their appearance. Any supermarket car park on a Saturday afternoon would see these two carrying the week's shopping to a ten-year-old Volvo estate. If you needed someone blend in, then these would be the two to do it, and perhaps that was their role.

She only had a vague idea of the structure of the outfit other than her job would essentially be the same as in the Met: gather the evidence and present the case. She knew there would be others assisting, but this was to be the core of the unit.

At the far end of the room the double doors opened, and two men entered. Leading, was Michael Strong, looking as good as ever. As soon as that thought entered her head she suppressed it. She was learning to cope and learning to be more circumspect with her relationships. He was strictly work, off limits, and was going to remain that way. As she caught sight of the second man her heart dropped, Chief Superintendent Brandon, her nemesis in the Met. She rolled her eyes and must have let out a low groan as the man next to her turned to see what was wrong. Brandon caught her eye and she was shocked to see him wink at her. What the hell was going on?

After a brief discussion with Strong, Brandon signalled for Helene to accompany him outside the room, through the double doors. Wondering if her career had ended before it started, Helene followed. Brandon let her go through first then closed the doors behind them.

"Helene, I owe you an explanation, and an apology."

She must have looked startled as he continued.

"First of all I apologise for pushing you so hard. I recommended you for this position, but I wasn't sure you would be interested given your dedication to the MIT. You are the best and we need the best here. The only way I could think of to steer you towards the job was to make you uncomfortable where you were. I really do apologise and hope you can forgive me. If there had been any other way, believe me I would have used it."

Helene's eyes narrowed.

"So you are part of this now?"

"I've been part of it since the outset, but I'm still employed by the Met. Coming from SO17 gave me access to some interesting information, people I wouldn't normally be able to reach. So when this group was first mooted, the powers that be decided I would be more effective keeping my current job and identifying both targets and recruits. What you see in there is the core. With the amount of work we have, we are going to need more detectives and operatives. We may even split into two teams." He gestured towards the doors. "Perhaps we should go back in and start the briefing. Michael can explain how this is going to work in far more detail than I can. It's his baby."

Helene tilted her head.

"And who exactly are these 'powers that be', Sir?"

Brandon shook his head.

"That, I'm afraid I can't tell you. Just suffice to say you are still in the employ of the UK government, indirectly."

Helene studied his eyes for a few moments.

"There something I need to say."

Brandon gestured for her to continue.

"You're a bastard." After a pause of several seconds, she added, "Sir."

Brandon let out a loud laugh.

"I suppose I deserve that and believe you me, you're not the first to say it."

Helene smiled. She thought she might get to like him after all.

CHAPTER SIXTY-SIX

The sight of a white crime scene tent greeted the early morning joggers and walkers on Wanstead Flats. Tomorrow, the murders would be front page news, but for today the passers-by stood and stared at the tent or completely ignored it; none of their business.

A constable, armed with a clipboard, kept guard in front of the 'Police' tape stretched around the scene. The path to the tent clearly marked with more tape.

Two figures emerged from a recently parked car, before donning crime scene suits and stepping briskly towards the scene. The constable noted their details on his clipboard before allowing them through; every person entering logged in and out. Trace evidence at the scene that couldn't be attributed to the investigators could belong to the perpetrator. The crime scene suits reduced the possibility of contamination.

Once inside, the purpose of the tent became clear. A large pit lay in the centre. Strong floodlights illuminated the horror below. One of the newcomers noted several partially covered bodies of what appeared to be young Asian girls. From the lack of decomposition, they couldn't

SIXTY-SIX

have been there long.

"What we got, Doc?"

Pathologist, Dr James Melbourne turned his head and raised an eyebrow. Even in that shapeless suit, he could recognise the shapely former DCI Helene Mackay, and there was no denying the draw of those deep brown eyes, examining him from beneath her hood.

"I thought you moved on, Helene? Where's DCI Matlock?"

Helene MacKay smiled behind her mask.

"In so many ways that's true, James. But I'm guessing a mass grave of young Asian girls is going to fall on my desk sooner or later, so here I am. DCI Matlock is no longer running the case, I am. Anyway, what are you doing here? This is a bit out of your area."

"Special request from high up, apparently. Running the case? I thought you left the Met?"

"I did, James. I'm now loosely connected to the National Crime Agency."

"Loosely?"

Helene smiled again. She had the first case for her new team and though he was not yet aware of it, she hoped she had her final member.

CHAPTER SIXTY-SEVEN

The officers studied the body in the alley. They'd been called to D and I, or so they thought. The guy wasn't actually drunk, but he was incapable owing to the fact he was dead.

"I know him. He's a small time drug dealer. Goes by the name of Donkey."

"What's that he's holding in his hand?"

The officer pointed to the bloodied pink object in the victim's right hand.

"It's his dick. The reason they called him Donkey."

The second officer turned and threw up against the fence.

"I'll call it in while you're making pavement pizza. Try not to contaminate the scene."

THE END

HARRY

Fishing for Stones
Glen R Stansfield

CHAPTER ONE
22nd February 1990, Near Longa, Angola

On the other side of the valley, five trucks were descending the steep slope to the bridge over the Cuiriri River: Russian built KrAZ. The convoy was still far enough away for them to get into an ambush position, and small enough for them to tackle.

The Major slowly lowered his binoculars, ensuring the sunlight could not reflect off the lenses and give him away to the enemy. Reconnaissance being their primary role, the standing orders still allowed for the attack of targets of opportunity, as long as it did not compromise their main duty of intelligence gathering. Under the cover of the tall grass he crawled up from the shallow foxhole, to where the rest of his group waited.

Parked on the opposite side of the ridge line, under a cluster of trees, the patrol's two 110 Land Rovers sat covered by camo netting to keep them hidden from occasional patrolling aircraft. They had chosen this place to lay up for a couple of days on the return journey to their operational base in Mavinga. With a clear view of the major highway between Menongue and Cuito Cuanavale, they observed the supply convoys passing between the two. Details of the movements would allow the intelligence unit to estimate the strength of the enemy in Cuito Cuanavale. This convoy was the first they had seen the Major thought small enough to be attacked by the eight-man patrol. He quickly briefed his men on its strength.

"Lead vehicle is carrying troops, fifteen at the most. The remaining vehicles are loaded with supplies. There may be someone riding shotgun in each truck but I can't tell at this range. We'll take them after the second bend this side of the river, a hundred metres west of where the trail joins the road. RPG to front and rear vehicles then mop up as necessary. Any questions?"

Several shakes of the head. They knew the drill. This would not be their first ambush. All were well trained, and they trusted the Major implicitly. He treated them well. Not like some of the other officers.

The heavily laden supply trucks used engine braking to slow them on the long descent to the river. The terrain in this part of Angola is characterised by a series of steep sided valleys cutting into a high plateau. Almost all the valleys run roughly north-south, carrying the rivers towards the Namibian border. The plateau is covered in a mixture of scrub, trees and grassland, some of the grass tall enough to hide a Land Rover, or even an armoured car.

On the other side of the river an equally steep climb awaited the convoy. The trucks would labour for several minutes until they reached the top of the valley, giving the group enough time to get into position for the ambush. Splitting into two teams of four they would position themselves far enough apart to be at opposite ends of the convoy as it passed. This would make it difficult for any survivors; the attack coming from two places, an effective tactic.

They left their camp and set off across the scrub towards a track leading to the main road; the grass kept down the dust. Once on the narrow track the convoy could not see them, which was just as well given the amount of dust they were now producing in their dash.

Although preparations seemed rushed, they had carefully chosen the ambush position. It was close to the camp with good cover on the north side of the road where they were, but little to the south. Situated between two bends, it was out of sight of any other vehicles there might be in the distance. They left the Land Rovers parked near to the highway under a tamarind tree, and close to the track. Ten minutes before the lead truck came into view around the curve; the two groups were in their respective ambush positions.

The Major breathed a sigh of relief; the vehicles still maintained their proximity to each other; exactly as he had observed them earlier on their descent. Far too close together in his opinion, making his task easier. The road dipped slightly here, and it provided an ideal location for the ambush. By hitting the convoy in this depression they had the advantage of elevation over the opposing force.

The RPG's fired simultaneously. A ball of fire erupted from the last truck as the round found its mark. At the front of the convoy things did not go as well. The Major watched in disbelief as the round from his own group's RPG passed through the open window of the truck. Under normal circumstances the downward trajectory from the team's firing position should have caused the grenade to hit the door on the other side of the truck, but by one of those strange twists of fate, one of the stabilising fins clipped the top of the window frame lifting the projectile enough for it to pass through the open window on the opposite side. Finally, the grenade exploded on a tree some thirty metres beyond the truck.

The KrAZ remained unscathed; the same could not be said of the driver. A second stabilising fin had sliced through the driver's neck severing the carotid artery and trachea in its passage; he was now drowning in his own blood. In his panic he stamped hard on the brake pedal. The back wheels of the truck locked up on the loose gravel and the truck slewed sideways across the road. Taken by surprise the following driver swerved to the right but could not avoid hitting the rapidly decelerating truck on the rear corner. The impact had sufficient force to tip it on its side. The complement of troops clung desperately to sides of the stricken vehicle but several fell onto the road. It finally came to rest, but not before one unfortunate soldier was crushed, trapped under the truck as it slid to a halt.

For a moment nothing happened. The world seemed to pause to take stock of the situation.

The thudding sound and high pitch whine of AK-47 rounds hitting the ground next to his head brought the Major back into the real world.

"Merda! Cubanos."

The Major ducked down as the rounds found their mark where his head had been a moment ago. A shower of earth landed on his helmet.

These were not the expected MPLA soldiers but some of the Cuban troops remaining in Angola. What on earth were they doing here? The Cubans should not be this far south as part of the withdrawal agreement.

Shots were coming from the lead truck, and the Major became aware of the sound of his own team's Heckler & Koch G3 weapons; the second team providing them with covering fire having quickly dealt with the surviving truck drivers.

The last thing he wanted was to get into a fire-fight, but things do not always go to plan.

"Raol, get that bloody thing reloaded and hit that truck."

A quick glance told him he needn't have bothered. Raol had already reloaded and was lining up the weapon on the lead vehicle again. This time the grenade hit the front of it with devastating effect. The troops taking cover behind were either killed or badly wounded.

The AK-47 fire diminished but did not stop entirely. A few of the Cubans had taken refuge in the ditch at the roadside, instead of by the now fiercely burning KrAZ, although being on lower ground had put them at a disadvantage. They had to break cover to see up the slope towards the attackers, but this did not stop them from firing back at the ambushers.

The Major thought there were maybe four or five survivors in the ditch, but the smoke from the burning trucks billowing into the sky was causing him more concern. It was time to withdraw before someone noticed the thick black plumes. Longa airfield had Mi-8 helicopters and in Menongue, further to the West, a MiG fighter squadron was stationed. He did not intend to be around when they arrived to investigate.

He signalled to the second group to withdraw to the Land Rovers. As he turned to his own team he saw Raol slumped on the ground bleeding from his right shoulder; conscious but clearly in shock. He gave instructions to the other two soldiers to get the wounded man back to the Land Rover. He provided covering fire as the men dragged Raol to the vehicles. Once they were clear the Major followed, firing short bursts towards the surviving troops on the road to dissuade them from attempting anything heroic.

Back at the Land Rovers, he learned one member of the second team had also been wounded. He had taken a round in the leg. Neither of the wounds were bad, but they needed attention soon. Luckily, in both cases, the bullet had passed through without hitting any major arteries or bone. He was not happy about it though. None of his men had ever been wounded before and he felt fully responsible and saddened.

Failing to destroy the lead truck had almost turned the attack into a disaster. Had it not been for the collision between the two trucks the Cubans might have reacted quicker and overwhelmed the small reconnaissance group. Only Raoul's quick reloading of the RPG had saved them from a difficult and protracted battle.

The Major surmised any searchers would be more likely to concentrate on the area to the south of the road, in the direction of the rebel stronghold. He elected to head west for several kilometres, on the north side and parallel to the highway, before turning south and home. It was a risky strategy; to the West was Longa and undoubtedly more Cuban troops, but he was certain the last thing they would expect was for his patrol to head towards them.

Thirty minutes later they crossed the main road without incident and headed south into the bush towards Mavinga.

He'd suffered enough of this. Whatever it took, the Major wanted to get out of this war, on his own two feet, and in one piece.

CHAPTER TWO

2nd March 1990, Boddam, Aberdeenshire

Three miles south of Peterhead lies the village of Boddam. Once a thriving fishing community, the village is now known more for the military installation of RAF Buchan, and the nearby Peterhead Power Station. In the harbour, the herring drifters and trawlers have given way to creel, ripper and leisure boats.

On the southern side of the village near to the military camp, and some sixty feet above the North Sea sits the former Earl's Lodge. In recent times it was a hotel until a fire destroyed the roof. Now it lies abandoned and in ruins. The building looks out on the rugged shoreline dominating the coast to the south of the village. Further to the South the cliffs sheer up from the shore, providing a breeding ground for seabirds. Below the hotel the cliffs are more accessible, and it is possible to clamber down the rocks to get nearer to the water; not the easiest thing to do when laden with fishing tackle, but the two men sitting there were regulars. A good place to fish unless foggy, then the problem is not the lack of visibility but the 'Buchan Coo'; the local name for the fog horn at the nearby Buchan Ness lighthouse. Although pointing out to sea, the horn is loud enough to deter all but the deafest of fishermen. It was not a concern today, the sun shone brightly, albeit without the warmth that comes from summer.

They sat each in their own thoughts, quite unusual for them as the conversation often flowed between the pair. Any subject could come under their scrutiny and they would discuss it at length.

The sound of the sea spilling against the rocks below, the Black Backed Gulls, Kittiwakes and a variety of other seabirds wheeling around the rocks and over the surface of the sea had Steve at peace with the world. He hadn't had a bite for over half an hour. Nothing unusual in this spot; quality over quantity was what this place was about.

"Steve, look!" Andy exclaimed suddenly breaking Steve out of his daydream. He pointed out to sea.

At first Steve couldn't see what he was showing him. Then he caught the glint of a windscreen or a wing. Two Hawker Siddeley Buccaneers were heading straight towards them low over the sea. They were so low they were level with Steve and Andy on the rock face. If they didn't gain altitude they could be the first men in history to be involved in an air accident whilst fishing. The two men watched as the aircraft approached and at the last moment pulled up to rise over the cliffs.

"Ho-leeee...!" The rest drowned out as four Rolls Royce Spey engines passed less than fifty feet over their heads.

The pair of them stood laughing with excitement.

"That first one was flown by Lieutenant Smythe, ye ken?" Steve said.

"How the hell do you know that?"

"I read it off his flying suit."

"Really?"

"Of course not ya muppet. I dinnae ken who's flying it."

"One of these days..." Andy said, laughing.

Steve and Andy had met two years previously at this same spot and hit it off straight away. Their friendship became stronger over the months. So it was only natural when Jane left Andy for someone else, Steve had been there to support him. He knew how difficult it was having gone through a divorce himself some years before he met Andy. Since then they had become like brothers. Now, they divided their spare time between flying, fishing, and another passion they shared: motorcycling.

"Things are not looking good at the moment," Andy said abruptly, sitting down again.

"Blue sky, fishing and a personal air show. How's that no good?"

Andy sighed, "I mean for me. Finances are a bit ropey. You know, since the divorce. I'm struggling to make ends meet."

"If you need anything let me know, anything at all. It's what mates are for."

"Cheers, Steve. I will."

They both lapsed back into silence.

Andy's rod tip suddenly shot down. "Whoa," he shouted grabbing the rod.

Five minutes later he landed himself a nice cod.

"Well, I'll be buggered," said Steve. "I've never pulled a cod like that out of here before. See, things are looking up already."

"Oh yeah. Just need to land another few thousand of these and my woes will be over," said Andy wryly.

"Is it that bad?"

"You've no idea mate," Andy said shaking his head.

"Bollocks, Andy is there nothing you can do?"

"I don't know yet, I'm working on it though."

CHAPTER THREE
13th March 1990, Jamba, Angola

President Dos Santos would have thought all his birthdays had come at once, had he been able to see the staff gathered around the table in the UNITA headquarters. A swift strike would remove the head of the UNITA beast and all his troubles would be over. Unfortunately for the President, he neither knew of the meeting, nor were his forces able to pinpoint the headquarters.

UNITA (União Nacional para a Independência Total de Angola) had once been an ally of the party now in power. In the days of the country's fight for independence from Portugal they had a common goal, to fight for a land free of foreign rule. Whilst they had a common purpose they put aside their differences. Once Angola gained its independence in 1975, the ideological differences between UNITA and the ruling party of the MPLA (Movimento Popular de Libertação de Angola) came to the fore. UNITA broadly followed the teachings of Mao, whilst the MPLA went along the Marxist route. These differences led the two sides to start a bloody civil war, one which had been raging for the past fifteen years.

The view of the UNITA leadership gradually moved away from the Maoist standpoint, declaring their sole intention was to see Angola as a country free of foreign interference. Democracy and socialism were still at the fore, but as the ties with the United States increased, the emphasis on socialism decreased. UNITA was aligning itself with the western world. On the other hand, the Soviet Union supported the Marxist MPLA, thus a cold war by proxy situation was born.

Dr Jonas Savimbi was concerned. Once again the leaders of the western world had called for a ceasefire in Angola, and once again funding and arms from these countries was in jeopardy. He did not understand how they could not see that to win this war he needed their support. He also did not see how the world was changing and Angola's Marxist fight was no longer a priority for them. Had he seen, he would not have cared in any case. His primary concern was to free his country, and he would do whatever he could to achieve his aims.

"Gentlemen, once again we find ourselves in a corner. This month I am to meet with the Secretary of State for the United States, and I fear he will not be bringing good news."

Several of the men seated around the table nodded in agreement.

"If we are to continue our struggle and finally achieve our freedom we must have an unbroken supply of arms and food. Any threat to cut off our supplies must be circumvented. We cannot allow the whim of a foreign government to decide our fate. I have gathered you all here today to look at ways of continuing to supply our troops with the equipment and food they need. Gentlemen, please speak freely and openly. Our very survival depends on this."

He looked around the room.

General Nunda was the first to speak.

"Will this mean our normal channels for purchasing arms will no longer be open to us?"

"I fear so. We must look for alternatives. We must also look for other ways to raise funds for our struggle. South Africa will follow suit if the United States cuts us off. We will no longer be able to sell our diamonds that way."

"Who amongst our allies will remain loyal?"

"A good question, and one for which I'm afraid I do not have an answer. Perhaps Zaire will give us support. I sincerely hope so," answered Savimbi.

"When it comes to arms, we are capturing much in the way of munitions and we have obtained several of the Soviet tanks, but of course these will not be sufficient for the longer term."

General Chindondo intervened, "In that case we must find another way to sell our diamonds and purchase the arms ourselves. Could we not sell them directly? It has a twofold benefit. We cut out the middle man and we can hide the source if we are careful."

Savimbi slowly nodded. "There is much merit in your plan, Wambu. But how do we sell? None of us have any experience other than through the South Africans."

"We have control of the mines, surely it is a simple matter of having someone from one of the mines sell on our behalf?" suggested Brigadier Ukuma.

"You would have someone we don't trust take a fortune in diamonds and sell them on our behalf, are you mad?"

The Brigadier lowered his head and nodded, conceding it would probably be a mistake.

General Nunda spoke once again. "I think I may have the solution to the problem. I have a young Major under my command. He is intelligent, adaptable and is a former diamond merchant."

"Have you indeed? But can he be trusted?"

"He volunteered to join us."

"We do not have to trust him entirely. I can send one

of my personal staff with him to make sure he returns with the money." General Chindondo said.

"It is an untried method. I think perhaps we should try this plan with a small number of diamonds, and if it succeeds then we can start to ship more this way," suggested General Chenda.

"Ben-Ben has a point, gentlemen," said Savimbi. "Perhaps we should try a small amount and take it from there."

Several of the men around the table murmured their agreement.

"Where is this Major now?"

"He's on a reconnaissance patrol at the moment. He's due back in a few days."

Savimbi lowered his head in thought then said,

"As soon as he returns have him report to Wambu to be briefed. Do not let him know why he has to report or who he is to report to. Have someone at one of the mines prepare a selection of diamonds for our young Major to look at. If he is as good as you think, he will confirm our own assessment and the plan can go ahead. Wambu, I want you to oversee this and ensure it goes well."

ooOoo

Fishing for Stones is available as an eBook, in paperback from all good book stores, and online. For further details, visit
www.glen-r-stansfield.com

FISHING FOR STONES

ABOUT THE AUTHOR

Glen R. Stansfield is a qualified aircraft engineer; a profession he has pursued for over forty years.

A lifelong interest in crime, in particular forensic psychology, led him to write his debut novel, **Fishing for Stones.**

When not writing, he can sometimes be found on two wheels, often using his motorcycle to raise money for charity.

His work has taken him to Bahrain where he lives with his wife, Jess.

He looks forward to your comments, good or bad, and you can visit him at:
www.glenrstansfield.com

Cover image © Glen R Stansfield,
Ysbrand Cosijn/Shutterstock (figure),
S.Borisov/Shutterstock (aerial view).
Set in Liberation typeface and released under the SIL Open Font License, Version 1.1. © 2012 Red Hat, Inc.

HARRY